He loves me,
He loves me not...

Pratibha Mishra

This book has been fully funded by the Wordit Art Fund.
Wordit Art Fund helps deserving authors publish their work by
providing monetary support. To apply for funding, please visit us
at www.BecomeShakespeare.com

First published in 2017 by
Becomeshakespeare.com
Wordit Content Design & Editing Services Pvt Ltd
Unit - 26, Building A-1, Nr Wadala RTO, Wadala (East),
Mumbai 400037, India
T:+91 8080226699

©
ISBN - 978-93-86487-41-4

DEDICATED TO THE LOVE OF MY LIFE...

THANKS FOR COMING IN MY LIFE AND MAKING IT WORTH LIVING.

THANKS FOR LOVING ME TO AN EXTENT THAT MAKES ME THANK GOD FOR ALL MY PAST BREAK-UPS.

THANKS FOR EVERYTHING BABY.

ACKNOWLEDGMENTS

Thank you "Patidev" for tolerating your "Biwi" who I know is not so easy to and thanks for loving me anyway.

Thank you Puneet sir for you will always be on the top of my

"ideal people" list.

Thank you Sandeep Pathak & Mark Fernandes (Mental), without you this book would not have been possible. Thank you for your incredible inputs on this writing piece and for making it much better.

Thank you Madhu for always being there with me. What else I can ask for after having a best friend like you? Thank you Bhawna for being my first reader and for your valuable inputs. Love you. Thanks to my all friends who have supported me when I was trying to get this novel published.

Thank you Neeraj my darling cousin cum friend cum advisor and what not. Thank you for always extending your hand whenever I am in need of it.

A big thanks to the team of "Wordit Art" for all the hard work you have put into this book's publishing.

And finally, a big thanks to the readers of this book for taking out your time to read it.

1.

Sometimes I wonder in solitude, if I am really so deeply loved by GOD ("Bhaggu"- as I like to call him for my own secret reasons) that I get so much of appreciation from all my bosses with whom I have ever worked that they all have recommended me for a promotion, at least once in my work span with them OR that he hates me so much that before I could actually grab that opportunity of promotion he creates a situation that drives me to quit that job unwillingly.

Sometimes I really feel like looking at him directly in the eyes and say "I hate you Bhaggu", but unfortunately for doing this heroic act, I need to die first in order to meet Bhaggu personally I guess, so I better choose to manage it with the idols of Bhaggu in temples only. But anyhow this not-being-able-to-grab-the-promotion is not the only reason for my hatred towards Bhaggu; there are plenty of them since I was a child of just 8 years of age.

It was 15th January of 2010, my father's birthday and the festival of Lohri which we used to enjoy a bit in the night being a close neighbour to a sweet Punjabi family.

It was a cold morning in Delhi and it was just my 3rd day at my new work place, The Russian Visa Centre where I was working as a Visa officer, though the designation sounds impressive, it was just an executive level post and nothing very exciting. The first best thing I loved about this job was that I had my two best friends working in the same office (Mansi & Bharti). The second best thing was that Mansi was to sit just next to me as she also had the same position. Mansi, Bharti and I used to live in the same area which gave us another opportunity to spend time together while travelling to and from office. Unfortunately Bharti had her shift timing of 10 am – 6 pm whereas mine and Mansi's was 9 am – 5 pm. So it was just me and Mansi left with our scooty-metro-walking gossips. We used to chatter all day long, starting with our meeting at our usual spot till we took our seats in office.

As it was off-season we were hardly having any work to do on that day. As usual me and Mansi were talking continuously when I got a call on my cellphone from an unknown lady who claimed to be the girlfriend of my then boyfriend. I used to get calls from her very frequently. I discussed this with my boyfriend and he said "just avoid her call, it's my cousin's wife who likes me". I did exactly same as I trusted him blindly. I looked at Mansi and turned the screen of my phone to show her that it's her call again. Mansi was a good friend of my boyfriend too and was equally charmed by his personality and sweetness. She asked me to avoid it. After avoiding her 7 continuous calls I got so irritated that I finally answered it to scold her to the death but as soon as I was about to utter out those maa-behan ki galiyaan, she confessed that she was not his girlfriend. At that very moment I was so proud of my choice and my trust on my boyfriend that I forgave her instantly for all her irritating acts, including those unbearable calls. I asked her not to call me ever again and she promised to do so but requested to meet me personally once before going away from mine and his life.

I discussed with Mansi and she said "call her to the office, we will meet her together". I followed what Mansi said and to our surprise in just 30 minutes that lady was in my office. I took her outside the office premises as I did not want to create any scene there, especially when I was a new joinee.

The lady looked beautiful. She had a short height but very thick and long hair. Anyone residing in Delhi could have guessed that she was a "Sikhni". I decided to give her 10 minutes to speak and then would tell her to go away. As soon as she started to speak she was full of tears in her eyes and I was full of mercy in my heart which made me listen to her non-stop for another 30 minutes.

She gave me some photographs and I headed towards my office, leaving her there in the stairway to wait for me. I had tears in my eyes as I seen Mansi. I cried... I cried like a kid. I was so loud that Bharti who worked across the floor in the other department rushed towards me and Mansi and asked what the hell is happening. What I told them sobbing was that my very honest boyfriend was a married man and the cute kid whom he used to address as his nephew was actually his own son. Mansi & Bharti reacted in the same manner as I did when I heard this. They shouted in unison "IMPOSSIBLE!!! That lady is a cheat and we are shocked to see you believe her instead of your boyfriend. I gave them those photographs, those were the marriage photographs of my boyfriend and that lady. Bharti & Mansi looked at me in disbelief.

They came out with me to see that lady and saw the cute little kid who was accompanying her, a sheer replica of my boyfriend. We were left with no words. That lady was kind

7

enough to understand that I was at no fault in breaking or at least on the verge of breaking her marriage as I had no idea of him being a cheater. I promised her that I would never like to see the face of that bastard again and apologized for unknowingly disturbing her married life. She left with a smiling face and left me with an I-so-hate-you-Bhaggu face.

Well, I could have surely gone into depression had I been an emotional fool and had I not have Mansi and Bharti around me at the time. It took me quite a lot time to realize that it all happened for good that I got to know the truth before it was too late. I started enjoying being single again and living a happy-go-lucky life. I even treated them both and termed it as a break-up party and we laughed on my stupidity and why did I trust him blindly that I never asked him how his nephew looked exactly like him. Indeed friends are blessings.

How freshly I remember every single minute of the day I had met Mansi & Bharti 6 years back in year 2004, when I joined the same school, they studied in. I was a tom-boy girl, very friendly, not very good looking but with attractive personality (as they said), very talkative, a leader in self and blessed with a good sense of humour. I was a short tempered girl, people who knew me well used to say that I can change my mood with just a blink of an eye. I could be heartly laughing at one second and within a blink of an eye I could be yelling from the core of my throat. Mansi & Bharti were childhood friends but were not in good talking terms for quite some time due to some family disputes as were neighbours back then.

As soon as I entered in my classroom of my new school, I spotted Mansi whom I had seen once in a friend's house who used to live near our home. I shook my hands with her and took a seat next to her. Mansi was an average looking and a

8

very sweet girl. She believed in simplicity and had loads of it in her. She had sharp features, very slim (slim to an extent that it was always a hot topic for my humorous comments), very reserved, shy in nature and very emotional sort of a girl. In short we were poles apart in our nature. I never thought she could be the girl whom I would proudly call "my bestest friend" one day and then entered Bharti in the classroom, gave me a how-dare-you-sit-here look and asked me to vacate the seat as she wanted to sit there. I looked at Mansi and she looked down. I vacated the seat instantly and moved but felt bad as it meant I will have to sit with some totally stranger now as I did not know anyone else in my new classroom, however it did not affect me much as I was sure that I will have a bunch of friends in no time, thanks to my friendly nature and who-cares personality.

Soon I was a friend to all my classmates but I chose to be close with 5 of them, naming Mansi (of course), Bharti (Unfortunately then, fortunately now), Babli, Somya and Vishakha. Unlike Mansi & Bharti who were in that school since 1st standard, Babli, Somya and Vishakha were as new as me. In no time six of us were famous in the school as "Cool Group".

Bharti was a fair and chubby girl who used to come school with a lot of oil poured on her head every day to get her a tight hairdo (which was another topic for my hilarious jokes), innocent to an extent that we had to explain her jokes after all the laughter in simplest language possible, which was more hilarious task than the joke itself when it was the case of a non-veg joke. She used to look quite boring at the first instance, but this was not the real Bharti. She had so much of fun inside that when she started showing her hilarious side and cracking jokes it was hard for anyone around to restrain her/himself from laughing.

Babli was a replica of mine. We shared a great bonding from the time I just said "Hi" to her. She was slim, average looking, fun-loving, friendly and just as talkative as me.

Somya on the contrary was a beautiful girl, very fair, stylish, reserved, had a short height but tall attitude. She was not a girl who talks to every tom, dick and harry. She did not like my carefree attitude when we first met and I did not like her oh-I-am-so-delicate attitude but eventually when we got to know each other better, we had to be not less than best friends.

Vishakha again was a very beautiful girl, fair and very talkative girl. We had a common friend who had studied once with her in a school and in a different school with me. So we became friends on the first day when we got to know this common friend fact of ours. To pen down all our stories that we have created in those 2 years of schooling I would need to write a whole new book. For now I need to come back to 2010 to start my favourite love story (My love story).

2.

After this my honest-turned-dishonest boyfriend incidence I started loving my single life more than ever before. As they all say "if you are brave enough to say goodbye, life will reward you with a new hello", I was finally over with my ex-boyfriend. It was so cool to not be answerable to anyone for your whereabouts. I was having a fun life with my friends all around. Then it was Bhaggu who wanted to play roller coaster again with me as it was his favourite time-pass I guess. It was another cold morning of winters in New Delhi when I and Mansi were gossiping and surfing through facebook in office with no work to do. We always had so much of time to talk as we used to spend almost 10-12 hours of a day together. I said pointing towards my computer screen showing Mansi a guy added in my friend list of facebook.

Look, what has he asked me in his messages? I said wearing a how-dare-he look.

Who? She replied trying to look with interest through her spectacles.

"Arey that uniform guy"

Wow! That navy guy…. What has he written? She asked with excitement.

Don't get so excited. He is asking me if I booze and go to disc and all. He is also asking about the night life that I enjoy here, in Delhi.

So, what's wrong in it?

What's wrong? How dare he to ask me if I booze? I have hundred of pictures in my albums, where the hell did he find me having a drink in or near my hand.

Oh ho, Calm down Pri. Aise hi puchha hoga, vaise uniform mein ladke kitne achchhe lagte hain na.... Let me add him too... I hope you would not be jealous, she said grinning.

Oh please, never again. I said with my hands joint.

I sent him a reply that read "Hi Arjun, I am fit and fine as always. Hope you are fine too. Well for your question, I do NOT drink; on top of that I do not like those people even who drink. I kind of hate Alcohol and Smoking. I of course go to disc to enjoy dancing with friends and the loud music ONLY. Nightlife here in Delhi is not as cool as your Mumbai, however I never go for night parties with friends as it is not allowed by my parents."

Arjun Tripathi, a guy from the dream city Mumbai. He sent me a friend request on facebook sometime back. An average looking guy, curly short hair, dark complexion, tall and an attractively heavy built. Well after that incidence I was too harsh those days to get attracted towards any guy for any reason. I added him just because I too liked his uniform which was a navy uniform. It was the picture of his ship where he was standing in his uniform at a place from where one could see the whole ship and the ocean around. We randomly shared messages on facebook as he was not very active on social sites.

After few days, I got a message from him asking for my contact number which I took as sheer flirting and got so angry that I removed him from my friend list without saying a single word to him. Days passed by and I was fully

12

engrossed with my family and friends in my life which was going smooth with a comfortable job. By then Bharti changed her job and joined a new company in Gurgaon, which did not affect me and Mansi much as Bharti was already in a different department and we could hardly get to talk to her in office hours except lunch break.

Months passed, it was the month of August when I again got a message on facebook from Arjun asking about my whereabouts. I too sent him a reply "I am perfectly fine dear, how are you". As soon as I clicked on sent button, I read our old conversations and realized why I had deleted him from my friend list earlier. I found it bit awkward to say anything rude after I have already sent him a reply with a "Dear" in it so I decided to just chuck it. After all it was my birth month and I was in a happy mood all month.

I had a BIG friend circle as I had gone to 3 different schools, had many friends in the neighbour and had worked for 4 companies before the present one. I was in touch with many friends from all the schools and work places. Apart from this BIG friend circle I was one of the naughtiest kids in my family. I used to get pampered by many of my relatives who loved me for my talkative nature, and then I had many cousins of my age who were not less than friends to me. This big circle made me feel very special on all my birthdays so August used to be my favourite month of the year.

It was a busy day at office as the season time had arrived. It seemed as if all the people of India were going to Russia and coming to us for their visa processing. I so badly hated every new faces I saw in my office with a bunch of documents in their hands. More than that I hated that idiotic supervisor of mine who did not even deserve to be a senior of anyone in the world, forget about me. He had very bad writing skills as

13

he was very poor in English, so he used to make me write all his emails and letters at the end of the day. I so hated to do his work after long tiring days. How badly I had cursed Bhaggu for giving me such bad luck that this type of man is being called "Sir" by me. Why could not he have let me grab any of those promotion opportunities in my previous companies? It was 5:15 pm by when I stopped cursing Bhaggu and left for the day.

Me and Mansi took a metro from Barakhamba metro station and were standing in front of a 6 seater desk, hoping for a good luck to get seats at Rajiv Chowk where the metro gets a relief for few seconds as utmost passengers get down at Rajiv Chowk and within few seconds the same metro gets double crowded with new passengers in it. We got one seat where I made Mansi to sit and hold my handbag too so that I could stand comfortably listening to my playlist with recently added new songs. I took out my phone from the pocket and started going through the facebook wall as a habit while travelling in metro, there were 8 notifications out of which 4 were for the request of some stupid games, others were for the comment of my friend's friends who commented on a photo/status where I had commented earlier. I ignored all and went to the message box where I had two unread messages. One from a friend, asking if I could help one of her friend with Canada visa details which I ignored again as I hated to think of any work after office hours. Second was from Arjun again. I smiled (do not know why, but I did).

He wrote, Hi Priyanka. Can I call you Pri? Priyanka is indeed a beautiful name but this Pri is easier to pronounce. Good to know that you are fine and you are not angry with me now though I was expecting a rude reply from you. By the way have any of your friends ever told you that you are too rude sometimes. That's bad; a pretty face like yours is not suitable

14

for rude looks you know. I did not notice that you have removed me from your friend list, I thought you are not replying because you might have got busy with your work as you once told me that April-August is your season time in travel trade. Anyways I just asked for your contact number because I am not very good in facebook, I rarely get to see it and when I am here, you are never online. Facebook is very slow medium for conversation. Also I am joining my ship tonight and will be out of country for next few months. I would not get a chance to check facebook for many days. Well, this was one of the reasons I wanted to stay in touch through phone and not just facebook. No offenses, hope you trust me. By the way, you can take my number if you are not comfortable in giving yours but mind you it will be an ISD number for next 4-5 months. See you. Take Care. Arjun Tripathi

I do not know why but I read this message twice.

I got so many things in minds to type for his reply but after reading his message once again, all I could type is my contact number with a winking smiley at the end. Shared this with Mansi and she smiled too. Next day evening I got a call from a strange number which turned out to be an international call, I answered it with my casual tom-boy tone. It was Arjun on the other line who had reached his country of destination and was waiting at the airport for his agent to take him to the ship. It was awkward at first to talk to a facebook friend on phone for the very first time but then we exchanged some formal talks as hi, how are you. He then asked for my email address saying it would be difficult for him to call frequently from the ship so he can always stay in touch with the emails. I gave him my email address thinking who the hell is going to check emails

15

As time passed Mansi also added Arjun on facebook and they also started chatting once in a while. I was sure by now that he also is among those guys who chase girls irrespective of the name, size, shape, caste etc. If she is a girl, nothing else matters. Once in the office I and Mansi were doing some random stuffs, facebook was one of them.

How do you think about Arjun? He has good sense of Humour, na?

Yeah, he is funny at times.

I think he likes you, she said trying to tease me.

Who the hell in this world cares if he does or does not, I said grudging.

That is rude. "Buraai kya hai ladke mein", she winked.

Well, there are a lot and I am not sure but I think he has been in a live-in relationship.

Mansi whom I had changed a lot from simple and emotional girl that she was once in our school days, was still a bit reserved. She replied with "sachchi?" bulging her eyes double than the size. I said I am not sure but I think he told me this once, also he drinks and smokes often. Upon hearing this Mansi created an ill image of him in her mind and avoided him as more as she could.

Later that day I checked my emails in my yahoo account and found an email from a strange looking email address, unlike yahoo, gmail, aol, hotmail etc. It was Arjun, second officer of some foreign ship. It was impressive. He wrote:

Hi Pri, sending you this email to let you know how to write

16

emails to me. Just type "To: 2/off Arjun" in the subject and it will reach me directly. Don't forget to change the subject everytime you write an email. Rest all is fine. Take care. Arjun Tripathi.

I was stunned. Does he really expect me to write him emails? Crazy man he is. I logged out. In the evening I and Mansi got down at our station which was Janakpuri west and took rickshaw for our residence. We were crossing our favourite adda for small parties, the C4-E market when we decided to stop to have a snack break. We chit-chatted alongwith our momos and lemon soda. I shared the email thing with her and we laughed. She teased me saying "lagta hai ladke ko hamari ladki pasand aa gayi hai". I smiled.

3.

Next day, Mansi was on leave and I was getting bored in the office whole day. I called Bharti as soon as I left office. We planned to meet at Ram Mandir near C4-E market. I reached before her and waited outside the temple. Being Tuesday there was a long queue of beggars who were waiting for visitors to give them the "prashad" to eat. I was noticing a 10 years old girl who was holding another 2-3 years old in her lap when I got a slap on my shoulders from back. Here she was, late as always. Bharti, her 5 minutes were always more than 15 minutes at least. She started blaming all the things of the universe like traffic, her driver etc for coming late until I stopped her. I told her to finish with the "darshan" soon as I was too hungry and wanted to go to C4-E market from there. Bharti used to visit this temple every Tuesday, She insisted me to join her in visiting the temple, which I rejected as always saying "I am still not on talking terms with bhaggu".

She went inside the temple and I as always used that time to have a butter scotch shake at the juice center, just in front of the temple. Soon after we were in market and had ordered our favourite momos with lemon soda, I shared with her about Arjun and his phone call and email incidence. With her typical confused look she asked me to stay beware as all she knew about navy guys was they all are big time alcoholics which made me avoid his email even more.

It was 26th August night and I was on the peak of my excitement as I knew many people on this earth were waiting for the clock to strike 12 so that they can wish me and go to sleep peacefully, however it was a different story at all that it was next to impossible for me to stay awake after 11 pm on any day. I don't like any disturbance when I am in the world of my weird dreams so I always sleep with my phone on silent. I even slept on all my real sisters' marriage, forget about being my birthday. What always made me feel excited about messages of 26th night was that it made my birthday morning very special. Finally the day arrived. I had a habit of checking my phone as the first thing to do after waking up and before leaving the bed with keeping the phone on charging. I had 3 missed calls, 2 from my best buddies Rakesh & Rajneesh who decided to drop me a message after I didn't answer their first call. 3rd was from an unknown number. Then there were plenty of messages with those copy-paste wishes, I typed a "Thank You" and pasted it for my reply to all.

I had an early morning bath, did some prayer for a change, touched feet of my parents and left for office. I had already planned my day's schedule in a way that I could meet most of my friends. I spent first half in the office and in absolutely no mood of work as it could have resulted in spoiling my party mood. Thanks to Bhaggu, I had Mansi as my colleague who promised me to take care of the work and boss when I planned to leave for celebrating rest of my day with other friends. I left and met a friend from my previous work place who never missed an opportunity to make me feel like a fool to refuse the proposal of a person like him, though he never proposed me directly. I spent my evening with few other friends watching a movie. Then as planned I met Mansi & Bharti for our just-girls dinner in Rajouri Garden. I received a call from an unknown and weird number while I was in the metro to my way to meet Mansi and Bharti. I answered and it was him again, Arjun. He wished me, I was amazed as I didn't expect him to remember my birthday as he was not very active on facebook but as it was a call from Philippines that too when he was on ship, I could not hear him properly and did not want to shout in metro. So I asked him to hang up as it was being difficult to hear him. He felt bad and I did not care.

I had given my scooty to Bharti that day so that she was not late again at least on my birthday with her same repeated excuses. Alas, she was late again. Being my birthday I did not scold her and hugged her as she started singing the birthday song in middle of the running traffic. We went to the restaurant, I had to cut the second cake which Bharti brought for me, we had dinner discussing my day and left for home, tripling on my love – my red pleasure scooty. The birthday was not over yet; I was welcomed in my home by my cousins, family and one of my childhood friends Anjna. She lived nearby. I was told to cut the 3rd cake of the day and we all enjoyed for some time. By the time I went to sleep, I had an ear to ear smile on my face. For a change, I thanked Bhaggu for blessing me with so many friends around and slept smiling.

One day during my lunch break, I was just checking my emails when I noticed that strange email address once again. It was a long email from Arjun. It seemed as if he had poured his heart in it. He wrote:

Hi Pri, You know as I have said earlier also you are very rude at times. You do not have any idea how difficult it was for me to find network on your birthday as I am in the mid sea on anchorage in Philippines. I was literally jumping in every corner of ship to find network to call you. First you did not answer my call when I called you at IST 12 and then when you answered it in the evening; you did not have even 2 minutes to talk to me properly. I am sure you must have not noticed my 2 missed calls also that you failed to answer in morning and afternoon. I would be honest with you. See I kind of have developed a feeling for you, of course after seeing your pictures on facebook, plus you too are a Brahmin like me. I also know these two facts are not enough for us to take this relationship any further or to even think about it, so I would like to know you more. I am not saying that I am already in love with you, what I am trying to say is I want to know you better in order to find out if you can be the girl I dream of having by my side. Rest all is fine here, waiting for your reply. Take care. Arjun

I was impressed by his honesty. Also was amazed to see how correct he was when he said I must have not noticed his unanswered calls during the day, I actually did not notice it despite of answering almost all calls on my birthday. Anyways, I replied:

Hi Arjun, received your mail. Hope the subject line is fine and this mail reaches you and no other Arjun on your ship. See, I quite liked your honesty so would like to continue that from my side too. I have recently been through a bad relationship after which I am hardly in mood of having any relationship before my marriage. May be this is one of the reasons of my rudeness. By the way, you are right. My friends say that I am the rudest and simultaneously the funniest girl of our group. I appreciate your efforts of doing all that on my birthday just to call me and I am sorry for my behaviour. Well I was really busy that day, you know with many friends to give time to; also it irritates sometimes to answer your call as I get my answer after almost 10 seconds of my question. Yeah I understand it might be because it is a long distance call that too with from somewhere middle of the sea or ocean but I do get irritated. Anyways hope you got your answer. Take care.

P.S – Only my best friend Mansi calls me Pri, for other

friends I am Pari or Priyanka.

I logged out as soon as I replied and shared this with Mansi. She gave her usual beautiful smile saying "I wish I was a Brahmin too" and winked.

Next day morning when I was yet to leave my bed, I was checking my messages. There was nothing that deserved a reply as I never liked to send those chirpy good-morning and good-night messages. I do not know what made me do that but I went to check my yahoo account and there it was. An email from Arjun, he wrote:

Hi Pri, sorry but I like this name for me to call you. By the way you never know you might want to call me your best friend one day. For your answer of having a recent break-off, all I have to say is "who the hell was that idiot who broke up with a pretty lady like you". Sounds flirtatious? Yeah I know your answer would be yes to support your honest (rude) character. Anyways on a serious note, you seem to be a practical girl of today's era. I do not think I need to tell you that all fingers are not same and for the mistake of one guy it is sheer foolishness to punish all. We can try to be good friends at least and mind you my few but fast friends say that I am gem of a friend to have and with your big friend circle I guess your friends must say same for you. You see, now we have a thing in common too. Take care and keep smiling. It hurts to see a beautiful girl sad (wink). Arjun

I logged out, kept my phone on charging and kept on thinking about this crazy guy while taking a shower till I met Mansi and we started with our non-stop talks about almost everything on the earth. Just after we had our lunch, I logged in to yahoo to reply to his email and it was when I saw another email from him. What's now, my mind asked and I started reading it for the answer.

He wrote:

Hey, forgot something in earlier email. Listen to a song "Anjane Chehre" of Raghav. Dedicated to you from me. Arjun

I could not restrain myself from finding the lyrics of the song on net. I googled "Anjane chehre lyrics by Raghav". The song suited our situation a bit with words like anjane chehre, guy from Mumbai, Pari etc. I instantly downloaded the song and replied him. I wrote:
Hi, thanks for dedicating the song but it is not that easy to steal the heart of this "pari". You are right, I am very much practical and do not intend to punish all the guys for the act of that one bastard, it is just that I am not in a mood of getting into a relationship again as I am enjoying this single tag. You see it gets you attention of many guys who are seeking for girls to get into relationship, like you (wink) and believe me it is great fun too but yes we can try to be good friends. Write something about you, your job, your family and friends etc in next email instead of throwing those flirtatious and cheesy lines. Kidding. Take Care.

Something came in my mind and I logged in again and wrote:
Well from me not the whole song but just a few lines for you from the song "ye ladka haye allah". The lines are "ho sakta hai dekho na, samjho mitti ko sona, pal bhar ka hasna ban jaye jeevan bhar ka rona, dekho jaldi mein kabhi dil ko na lagana, ktna mushkil hai tauba isko samjhana ke dheere dheere dil bekaraar hota hai, hote hote hote pyar hota hai, ye ladka haye allah kaisa hai deewana" (wink).

It was a Saturday and just half working day for me and Mansi and full day off for Bharti, Kapil and Rakesh. Me and Mansi had planned a movie with three of them. Ever since I finished schooling, I wasn't in much contact with Somya and Vishakha as they didn't live nearby or worked nearby too. I did not meet them often, only once in a while. So my very close friends with whom I shared almost everything were these people only. Rajneesh was another good friend but he had shifted to Bangalore for his job. We had a great time having lunch together followed by movie in Rajouri Garden. We three came back doing tripling again on my scooty escaping all the traffic cops (thulle).

As soon as I entered in my home my mom started her radio (oh, did I tell you that I call my mum radio mirchi with love). She shouted – I don't understand why you always come late on Saturdays whereas people generally have off or at least half day on Saturdays. Well I had not told her that my every alternate Saturday was a half day so that I could enjoy at least two days of the month with my friends without any tension of home and office. I made excuses of having lots of work on Saturdays as the next day was a Sunday. My mom had shifted from Ranikhet, Uttarakhand to Delhi only after her marriage and having 5 kids (4 daughters and 1 son). Being the eldest daughter of my grandparents she did not get to study much in the village but for us she was very intelligent and it was very hard to fool her. So she knew it very well that I am just lying and that I spend my Saturday evenings with my friends.

After a non-stop lecture of almost 15 minutes, she got indulged in her domestic chores and I in my television. My mom shouted from kitchen "colours laga, balika vadhu aane wala hai" which I instantly followed as I was in no mood of getting an another 15 minutes lecture. She came in drawing room with her vegetables to be chopped off and started

24

watching her serial. I was getting bored so I logged in the yahoo expecting a reply from Arjun. There was nothing which made me disappointed. It was fun chatting via emails for a change. I surfed through facebook, went to his profile and scanned it. He did not write much about him. He had very few pictures of his own, those too with the friends only. No single photo of his to have a closer look. I logged out. It was time to go to sleep, I checked yahoo again. No mail yet, I slept disappointed.

Every Sunday was a busy day for me as my sisters who were married always came home for lunch with their kids. As always both of them kept cursing some or the other person in their in-laws and my mom consoling them saying "sasural hota hi hai aisa, teri daadi kaun sa kam thi, wo bhi aisi hi thi" followed by her own sad story. I met Mansi and Bharti in the evening and went out for a short scooty ride to C4-E. By the time my sisters left, we were all tired and buried ourselves in the bed. It was Monday morning and after checking the text messages, I automatically went to yahoo and there it was, a very long email from him which I kept unread for reading in office as I was already getting late for the office.

It was a very comfortable job that I had with a limited time of work. Our work was to accept visa applications between 9 & 12 and to deliver back the passports with stamped visa between 3 & 5. Applicants used to come between 10 & 12 generally which gave us 1 hour of 9 to 10 to do our own personal work enjoying the morning tea. Same with the evening as we were free after 12:30 generally and until 3 pm we had work for the name sake only. It was 9:15 when I got settled with switching on my computer and keeping the lunch box in the hotcase. I logged into yahoo and opened his email. He wrote:

Hi Pri, see we have got another thing in common, we both are witty. Well about me, I am 3 years older to you (which can be a perfect match, wink). My roots are from Bihar but I have been staying in Mumbai since my childhood. I have two sisters out of which one is married and settled in Mumbai itself and one brother. I am the youngest in all siblings. My mother is a home-maker, father was in dockyard of Indian Navy and has got retired last month only. My eldest sister is a home maker taking care of her two little kids (a son and a daughter), her husband runs several educational institutes of his own. My second sister is teaching in a reputed school of Mumbai, we are looking for a match to get her married. My brother also is in merchant navy like me and holds the same position of Second Officer. My father wanted me to go into engineering but I chose to be here, in the Merchant Navy. I am preparing for the next level, so I will be soon getting designation of Chief Officer. Unlike you I have very limited friends, naming Rajesh, Sandeep, Abhiraj, Ajeez & Amrita. I occasionally drink & regularly smoke. Earning good and have recently bought a 2 BHK in Mumbai where we are going to shift soon as right now we are staying in navy apartments. No girlfriend at present, though had a few in the past but was not serious for any of them and I guess neither were they. I think that's all about me. Let me know if you want to know something else. Listen another song from movie Gajini "hai guzaarish", dedicated to you. Write about you in the reply, will wait for your email eagerly. Take care. Arjun

I read the email again; he seemed to be an honest man though it made me feel obvious that he can never be my match as he had those two wonderful qualities of drinking and smoking that I hated from the bottom of my heart. I downloaded the song and decided to listen it in the metro on my way back. Mansi had an argument with our senior that day so she was in full anger whole day. I decided to calm her down by promising a C4-E visit on our way back to home, I even asked Bharti to be there on time. I plugged in my earphone as soon as I entered in Metro taking a safe corner to stand comfortably. It was a nice song with meaningful lyrics which gave me something very similar to butterflies in the stomach. The feelings were strange but I did listen to the song at least 3 times before getting down from the metro. The lyrics were as follow:

"Sheeshe ke khwab leke raaton mein chal raha hoon, takra na jaun kahin.
Asha ki lau hai roshan fir bhi toofan ka darr hai, lau bujh na jaye kahin.
Bas ek haan ki guzaarish, fir hogi khushiyon ki baarish.
Tu Meri adhoori pyaas-pyaas, tu aa gayi dil ko raas-raas
Ab toh tu aaja paas-paas, hai guzaarish.
Hai haal toh dil ka tang-tang, tu rang ja mere rang-rang
Bas chalna mere sang-sang, hai guzaarish.
Keh de tu haan toh zindagi, chainon se chhoot ke hansegi
Moti honge moti raahon mein.
Tu meri adhoori……..

Mansi had started cursing our senior as soon as we got down at Janakpuri metro station, took scooty from the parking place where I used to park my scooty daily and reached C4-E in 5 minutes. As always we had to wait for 20 minutes for Bharti to come. Mansi was an innocent girl so even her abuses did not go beyond kutta-kamina which made me and Bharti laugh hard. Mine and her way was same for taking out our anger on seniors by spitting out all the abuses on their back that girls are never supposed to use. Bharti was having a crush on her ex-colleague those days that I also knew as I and Bharti had worked for the same company two years back. She was then working for Italy visa centre and I for Dubai, both centres belonged to the same parent company.

27

This guy was a colleague of Bharti in the same centre. He was so cute that I and Mansi did never mind hearing Bharti's crush stories.

It was 9 pm of the same day and my time of making chapaatis with music in the kitchen. I had a habit of doing household works with music only. It made those boring chores interesting a bit though I mostly worked on Sundays only. Sunday was official off day for my mother and for us off officially but working day at home. I played "hai guzaarish" and continued with my chapaati making session wondering if this guy is really so desperate to hear a "Yes" from me.

Next morning as soon as I got free time, I started typing my reply for Arjun. I wrote:

Hi Arjun, it was nice to know about you. Well for me, I belong to Uttarakhand (land of God) but reside in Delhi with my family since I was 3 years of age. I have 3 elder sisters (all are married and have kids) and one younger brother. My maternal uncle also stays with us in our home, he is the youngest brother of my mother. My two elder sisters are settled in Delhi itself, the third one is in Pilani, Rajasthan. My mother also is a home-maker and my father is a retired person like yours. My brother is younger to me and he is studying right now, he is doing his software engineering. I always wanted to be an air-hostess since my childhood but my father did not like the profession so he said no for it, then after getting many comments cum compliment from my people around that I debate quite well, I decided to go for journalism which this time my mother did not like saying it is a risky job for girls. By the time I could have decided what exactly to do after 12th my father took voluntary retirement due to some unavoidable issues running in his office. I had already taken admission for my graduation in Jesus & Mary College of Delhi but opted to do it non-regularly so that I could look up for a job simultaneously. Well being just a 12th passed that time I had to start with a domestic call centre, after few months I joined an MNC, a travel company with Bharti. Since then I am working in this same sector and right now serving the Russian Visa Centre. By the way now I have completed my graduation and currently pursuing my Masters in public relations & advertisement. I am also doing L.L.B and am in the first year of it. For friends, I have a lot of them but Mansi, Bharti, Vishakha, Somya, Rakesh, Kapil, Rajneesh and Anjna are my best friends. Take care.

The problem in our email conversation was if I wrote the email in a
morning, I knew that Arjun will be receiving it by the afternoon and his reply I will be receiving in the evening or at the night.
Email system on his ship was that slow. We left exactly at 5 pm from the office and I had already planned to take "samosa" (mine and my father's favourite) with me for all in the family. I reached my home at around 6:15 and hated for getting this wonderful thought today only as I encountered my cousin's husband just after entering in the drawing room who came to visit us. I called him "jiju" in his front and bastard behind him. He was the reason behind my tom-boy nature as it was him because of whom I hated the fact that I was a girl. that too when I was just 10 years old. Even today I get anger rolled in tears in my eyes when I think of that horrible night. Sometimes I feel, I could not do or say anything that night for I was too small to take any stand but what's now. Why don't I just go and strike his head with a hammer in dark someday. Well imagination of doing this gave me a mischievous smile; it would have been the greatest achievement of my life.

29

I messaged Mansi if she can come out for a walk as I was not willing to spend any more minute in the home till the time he was there. As always she refused to come out after entering in the home due to her arrogant dad who never missed an opportunity to interrogate about her being out. I started my scooty and parked it outside her home. Mansi went to make tea for us when I decided to check if Arjun has replied to my email. He had replied and it was like:

Hi Pri, you know since the day I saw you on facebook while I was looking for some other Priyanka (a girl from my colony), I always knew there is something very special about you that I could not stop myself from approaching you and forgetting that Priyanka. I must appreciate that at such a young age you have taken so many responsibilities on you. I understand being an only earning member of the family that too by a girl at this age is really not that easy. I am impressed, well I always was. You are a real gem of a person, working along with studies since young age, unlike girls of your age, much more mature and responsible.You have left me speechless but I would still like to say something. I have decided, I do not need any more time to know or understand you. I never approached you with the plan of dating or having an affair, I think I am too old for that. You are among those girls who are counted as perfect marriage material. I am sure any guy of your friend circle would love to marry you and I am one of those. You take your time to know me, understand me and do whatever you want to do but I have just one request. Please give me a reason before saying "No" and give me a chance to explain. A song dedicated to you directly from my heart. "Zara si dil mein de jagah tu" from the movie Jannat. Take Care. Arjun

I was lost when Mansi came with the tea and asked. What

happened that made you left home just after 10 minutes of reaching there? "Pehle bolti to ghar hi nahi aate na, C4-E ghoomte. Ghar aane ke baad ye baapu kahin jane nahi deta pata hai na tujhe". I did not answer so she sensed that something was serious. She asked what happened and I showed her Arjun's email. She sighed with relief after reading and said, you scared me idiot. It is just a proposal and you are reacting as if someone has sent you an atom bomb in the email. By the way "kya socha hai?" I replied, what is there to think. This guy has everything that I would never want in my would-be husband except a handsome salary which alone is not enough for me. I will straightaway say a NO in my reply. She said if I am sure of my answer, why I am worrying so much then. I agreed with her and started sipping my tea and bitching about the girl next door.

I reached home and fortunately the monster was not there then. I started with my chapaati session when I played his dedicated song. It was again a romantic song where the guy was requesting girl to allow him to enter in her heart as he loved her enormously. I could not stop myself from replying Arjun as I did not want him to hold any false feelings. I wrote:

Dear Arjun, I think it is going too far now. I like you for your honesty and do not want you to keep any false feelings from my side. See being very honest we have no match, in many terms which I don't want to explain. Please excuse me and take this email as a NO from me. Take care.

I sent this email and slept thinking of him, his email and his dedicated song. First thing I did in the morning was to check my yahoo and there was an email from him. I could not wait to see his reaction. He wrote:

Hi Pri. You broke my heart brutally but I appreciate your straight forward nature. Achchha listen I cannot force you, all I want you to do is to please explain those terms where we don't match. Now don't take it personal, I just want to know all those so that I can improve myself wherever required so that the next girl I propose should not say NO. I hope it is not because of my looks as it is difficult to improve that, and remember I asked you to say No with reasons only. Hope you will help your friend. Take Care. Arjun

4.

I was relieved for he was not that hurt as I expected him to be. So I replied after reaching office.

Hi Arjun, see all girls are not same so it is not that if I have said no, all of them would say no. For my reasons of saying No to you are...
1) You drink (I hate that),
2) You smoke (I hate that too),
3) You are from Bihar (My parents would never agree for this match),
4) You stay in Mumbai (I love Delhi and do not want to leave it at any cost),
5) You have been in a live-in relationship (too high of a thing for me to accept)
6) We are very different with our financial status; you are too rich to marry a girl of my standard.
7) I am not as good looking as I seem to be in my photographs (as my friends say, It is because I am a bit photogenic).

P.S – My NO is not because of your looks as looks do not matter to me. Take care.

In the afternoon, my boss called me in his cabin and asked if I would like to shift from Visa department to Hotel department for which I asked time to take decision on. I was discussing the same with Mansi after returning back to my seat when our office boy Devendra intervened with a suggestion "madam galti se bhi mat chale jana uss department mein. Thodi si salary badhayenge lekin target de deke jaar nikaal denge. Achchhi khaasi job chal rahi hai padhaai ke sath, karte raho isey hi". He was right as same thing had happened with Bharti too. She decided to shift to

Hotel department after knowing the salary and scope is better there and resulted in leaving the job just after 6 months of her transfer.

I said "No" to boss for the transfer giving xyz reasons but inside feeling proud for keeping my tradition alive of being offered a promotion in all my workplaces.

In the evening I had received a reply from Arjun, it was like:

Hi Pri, thanks for accepting my request and elaborating your refusal. On your 7 points what I have to say is as below:
1) Yes, but I am not alcoholic. I do it occasionally in parties etc (if you do not like it, I can quit that).
2) Yeah but I am not a chain smoker (will quit it too if you say).
3) Parents part you leave on me, I will talk to them and handle.
4) Reason of me staying in Mumbai is childish. You know even if you marry a guy of Delhi, you may have to shift to some other city for his job or any other reason.
5) I have been in a live-in relationship and I don't know that? I mean when and with whom and most importantly who told you this?
6) Point of the status is childish again, that does not matter anyway.
7) Looks are no problem to me. And yes, I also don't look as bad as it seem in my photographs (as my friends say, It is because I am not at all photogenic).

P.S – I will call you tonight, we are at a port and the network is fine here in Australia. Stay free at 9 pm IST. Take Care. Arjun

I started typing the reply but then deleted as soon as I

realized we will be talking on phone tonight. I shared everything with Mansi.

I think Arjun is right Pri, except his drinking and smoking issues, all your points are non-sense.

You know Mansi, I think I have kind of started liking him.

Finally!

What do you mean?

Of course you like him, your face, your body language, except your mouth, everything says you do. Talk to him on phone and see if things can really work between you guys.

I asked my mom to make dal-chawal that night so that I don't have to make chapaati and get time to talk to Arjun when he calls.

Arjun called at sharp 9. I answered it saying "very punctual" and he replied I was waiting for the clock to strike 9 since last 30 minutes. His voice was very attractive, very macho and full of confidence. There was a moment of lull and then he spoke again. I hope there is no disturbance in this long distance call today to irritate you.

I replied, no it's much better today. He then said, so that last email was from me so I guess it's time for you to speak. I started saying see Arjun, my father has been drinking ever since I know him. He has tried to quit it number of times and failed, same with my chacha ji and dada ji (uncle & grandfather). You can't even imagine how much I hate this habit that I don't even keep those friends who drink as because of it my family & I have suffered a lot. Smoking is even worse for this I know, it is next to impossible to quit it.

35

He answered as he sensed a feeling of hurt in my voice. Pri I am not alcoholic, trust me I drink occasionally which is very rare. I can quit it today and if you ever find me doing this you can leave me without any notice. For smoking yes you are right, it is very difficult to quit it but again it is not impossible. I know it's harmful for my own health, if you are with me I would love to quit it, though it will take some time. Give me a chance at least. I then said – It is not that easy to convince my parents. Firstly they are not in favour of love marriages even if they are within the caste, different culture and caste is out of the question. My elder sisters were told to leave the house when they fell for two guys in our neighbourhood. He said, leave that on me. I will talk to them and trust me they will accept our relationship. By the way what about this live-in thing, he asked. I replied hesitantly I don't know but I think you only told me this when we started to chat on facebook. He replied, show me that chat and I am ready to lose anything. You might have heard it from some other friend. I accepted and said sorry for that as I too had tried to find this chat of live-in relationship once to show Mansi but could not find it. He then said, now the only point remains is of financial status. What is wrong with it? You are an educated girl, you earn and run a family, you are confident enough to live an independent life. What else is required? I replied, it is not about being independent only. Since the day my father has taken voluntary retirement, I am the only earning member in my home and I also don't get a very handsome salary. My annual salary is more or less equal to your monthly salary. My father has not saved a single penny for mine or my brother's marriage. Whatever he earned through a private job, he has spent for upbringing his 5 children in a metro city, buying a big home in Delhi and in marrying his 3 daughters with all the customs. I am saving from my own salary for my marriage as I don't want to burden my dad with any sort of loan for my marriage. He said, that is very impressive of you, but if you are worrying about dowry and all, rest assure it is no problem at all as I am against dowry. I interrupted saying what about your family. They must be expecting something from the family of their would-be-daughter -in-law. Sorry but I know my family a bit more than you, he said throwing sarcasm, they too are not in favour of dowry. And as you said I earn pretty well so I do not care how much you earn.

See Pri, every problem has a solution if we are ready to face it. I think that was more than enough for today. You take your time for thinking about this relationship. All I have to say is "I will never let you repent your decision of choosing me if you give me a chance". I really love you. I wished him good night and said good-bye avoiding his last line. He wished me good night too and hung up.
I went to bed repeating all the conversation in my head and finding it difficult to sleep. I logged into yahoo and wrote him an email. I wrote:

"Ajanbi mujhko itna bata, dil mera kyun pareshan hai.
Dekh ke tujhko aisa lage jaise barso ki pehchan hai"

Next day morning was different; I was already feeling as if I am in love. I slept thinking of him, had dream of him and woke up thinking of him. Checked my email in office and there was one. He wrote:

Hey, would like to dedicate you some lines of your song ye alllah haye allah… … "Bholi ho tum kya jano, ab bhi mujhko pehchano, Sapna tumhara main hoon, mano ya na mano"… Hope I did not hurt you with anything I said yesterday but it is so good to hear your voice that I feel boring writing this email but I know you must be in office and busy with work. I will call you tonight at around 8 pm. Try to keep urself free at that time. Take care. Arjun

I replied:

Hey Arjun, before we talk again I want to share few things with you. First - In 2004 I slipped down from our stairs of first floor and landed directly on the ground floor which caused me a crack in spinal cord. I was in hospital for 15 days and then they advised me a bed rest of 3 months which I did not follow and started moving from one and half month onwards as I had to give my final exams of 11th standard. I did not want to leave my friends for if I would have failed to give those exams, they would have left me behind in the same class jumping to the 12th. I simply could not afford that and gave exams and passed, but failed in giving a proper treatment to my very own self. In one visit to the doctor, he told me something that I think I should probably let you know. He told me that there in the spinal cord is this crack only and not a fracture that they could have cured. He asked me to avoid lifting heavy weight, avoiding rough travel and most importantly PREGNANCY as it can affect the crack and turn it into fracture during pregnancy which can be dangerous. It has been long but I am not sure if the risk is still there or not. Second thing that I want to share with you is that I was almost raped by my cousin's husband when I was just 10 years of age which has left me getting irritated by whispering sounds and scared of getting physical. I don't know when I will be getting rid of my fear or I will ever be able to do that or not. Third thing – As you know, I have recently been through a bad break-up and ugly relationship. It will be hard for me to take another now, so just in case you want a timepass, I would sincerely request you to find that in your own city and spare me. Bye

I logged out and moved to the washroom and cried silently

thinking of all the negativities that I had around me. I cursed Bhaggu for everything. Mansi noticed my sadness as soon as she looked into my eyes. She was one such darling who always knew what condition I am in. She asked and I shared everything with her. Why me all the time. Why in the whole world I only could not follow my dreams, I said. She consoled me saying see God has given you all the pains as he knows you are brave enough to handle all that and blah-blah that made me stop crying and being the centre of attraction in the office.

We went to Pizza hut that evening to evade my bad thoughts. We parked our scooty in district centre and headed towards pizza hut. After the pizza, we spent some time in wandering around and ended in buying some random stuff from the craft market.

I was walking on my terrace when Arjun called at 8 sharp. I answered wondering if he had already received my email and read it. What would be his reaction?
He said hello.
I replied with a lame "Hi".
Received your email, he said.
Then what do you have to say on it, I asked.
You scared me when I first started reading it but you disappointed me. I was expecting something like I am HIV+ or something more dangerous, he joked.
It is not at all funny Arjun, these are few of those reasons for why I hate Bhaggu so much.

Who? Bhaggu. Who is it? He asked.

I mean God, I explained.

Oh, that's such a cute name. God and Bhagwan sounds so

formal, isn't it? Bhaggu sounds as if we are talking to or about a friend, he said laughing.

It irritated me so much that I hung up without a single word and when I was on my stairs to go down he called again.

Ok, I am sorry. Listen the three things you shared with me have not affected my feelings for you and trust me I am falling deeper and deeper for you with every passing day. He started speaking without knowing if it was actually me on the other side of the phone or not. Well fortunately it was me.

He again spoke. The first thing you told about that unfortunate accident, it is sad but who the hell was that doctor who interpreted about what will happen after 10 years. Anyways that too is not a big deal, I am sure it can be cured. All I can do is to promise you that we will get it fully cured first and then only will think of family planning. Second about your cousin's husband I don't have enough epithets in my vocabulary for him. How dared he? Trust me if I will ever see him in the future I will punch him in the nose. Thirdly, about looking for a timepass, only TIME can prove me right and honest. I know whatever I may say today you are going to doubt me and I truly understand your situation. All I have to say is please give me one opportunity to prove myself. Now would you say something here or will write in the email once I hang up, he asked laughing? I laughed too. I did not know if whatever he said was true or not but I loved every word of him. It was 9 when I noticed the time and asked him to excuse me as it was time for me to perform my one and only help of the day to my mother. He asked me to write whatever I have to say and I agreed. I love you, he said in response to my "Bye" and I disconnected saying "Thank you".

I kept repeating his words until I got free time to write him an email after the dinner. I wrote:

Heart says, I should trust you, mind argues. I am confused. All I can say is thank you for making me feel so special. You were right when you said only time will prove what is right and what is wrong, what's true and what's false. Still I would suggest you to meet me first, look at me in the real and then decide if you are sure of your decision. Mind you, I am not that beautiful as you expect. And yes, I forgot to tell you one more thing, I can't cook. Apart from being a master in making chapaatis all I know is how to cook rice, maggi and tea. Now what solution you have for this (wink). Cya

I slept peacefully that night thinking of how we would react when we will actually meet. Will he be able to win my heart or vice versa? What if he does not find me good enough to keep his promises? What if he also realizes that I look nice in the pictures only? For the first time I cursed myself for being photogenic and slept blaming Bhaggu for it.

It was a routine now to check yahoo first avoiding all text messages. He had sent an email which I had to keep unread as I was late again for the office. I hated it. I was dying to park my scooty and enter in metro so that I could read his email. By the time we climbed stairs and reached platform, a train was about to shut its' doors. I ran towards it and succeed to enter but in the excitement I forgot to check if Mansi has boarded the metro or not. She didn't. I called her immediately realizing my mistake and told her that I will get down at next station and will wait for her. I started reading the email while waiting at the next station. He wrote:

Hey Pri, I suggest you listen to your heart as some great person has said once "The heart is at left but it's always

right" and I don't care if you can cook or not, I need a wife not a chef. But yes as I have said many times that every problem has a solution and I am a firm believer of this saying. We will order sabzi-dal from the restaurants and you just make chapaati, you know Mumbai is famous for having at least one restaurant in every street of it. Pri it does not matter if you are as beautiful as you look in your pictures or not, I love you for who you are. I don't know what but there is something very special about you, about us that too from the day I have seen you on facebook, I am sure of having you next to me as my wife one day and
I will prove it right.

Today I want to promise you something....

I promise to be a gentleman

I promise to be understanding

I promise to be mature

I promise to be a good friend

I promise to be only yours

I promise to be caring

I promise to be with you always

I promise to be a support always

I promise to make u smile always like this (I hope you are smiling right now)

And just like all these promises, my promise to you is, to

LOVE YOU truly, madly, deeply, intensely and infinitely.
Arjun

I loved his email and read it as many times as I could. I replied with just a "Thank You".

5.

Meanwhile my mother was in a very sweet mood that day. I asked her what happened, and she told me that my uncle from Pilani had suggested a match for me. She said he is an engineer and currently working in Australia. His parents are living in Pilani just next to my uncle's home. I did not know how to react, I got numbed. My mom sensed it and asked if there is someone I already like. I was not sure if I should tell her anything about Arjun as even I had not met him personally and was not sure if he will be the same Arjun after meeting me. I replied, no it's not that. It's just I am not ready for marriage yet, I am just 24. She replied "itni si baat? Hum kahenge na ladke walo se ke ladki ki masters complete hone tak ruk jao". I didn't say anything but nodded and she left smiling as if she needs to start the preparations right there.

I wanted to discuss this with Arjun so I desperately waited for his call. He called a bit late at around 10 when I had just finished my dinner. I answered it after reaching my terrace.

Why are you calling so late today? I sleep by 10:15 usually. I said
I am so sorry but got really busy with work today. Now please don't say you can't talk as you are sleepy. I actually was but as I too wanted to speak to him I denied. After some formal talks, I told him what was cooking at my home. He got much serious than me. After a pause he said, fine. I will come to Delhi directly after my signoff. I want to meet you ASAP so that I can get your final answer which is pending for a face-to-face meeting. I interrupted asking what about you?

He replied – what? My decision is final. I want to marry you and that's it.

But I can't be assured until I meet you. I said in anger.

Ok-ok, calm down. That's why I want to come there ASAP so that there is no doubt at all. I am coming back next month, may be around 20th December. Will stay there for 4-5 days and then leave for Mumbai.

What about your parents? Will they allow you to? I asked.

Well, I will have to lie as they expect me to enter in home first as I will be coming back after 4 months. That's ok. I will manage that. You stay ready with the plan as you have to be my guide for my Delhi tour. Oh god, I am so excited.

Me too, I chuckled.

Achchha, listen this song, "Dil ibadat". Every word of the song is dedicated to you with all my heart.

Ok Bye. I am really sleepy now, I will talk to you tomorrow. I said and hung up with a "Thank You" in response to his "Love you".

I buried myself under my blanket and played this song in my phone with earphone plugged in.

"Dil ibadat kar raha hai dhadkane meri sunn, tujhko main kar lun haasil lagi hai yahi dhun.
Zindagi ki shaakh se lun kuch haseen pal main chunn, tujhko main kar lun haasil lagi hai yahi dhun.
Jo bhi jitney pal jiyun, unhe tere sang jiyun, jo bhi kal ho ab mera, usey tere sang jiyun.
Jo bhi saansein main bharun unhe tere sang bharun, chahe jo ho raasta usey tere sang chalun.

45

Dil ibadat..........
Mujhko de tu mit jane, ab khud se dil mil jane, kyun hai ye itna faasla.
Lamhe ye fir na aane, inko tu na de jane, tu mujh pe khud ko de luta.
Tujhe tujh se tod lun, kahin khud se jod lun, mere jism-o-jaan mein aa, teri khushboo odh lun.
Dil ibadat........."

It was a nice track and I had heard this song many times, but it never felt so special to me before. I shared everything with Mansi and Bharti. They asked me to make sure that he meets them too. I agreed as I too wanted them to meet him and give their opinion on my choice.

It was the afternoon when I received a call from Arjun next day. I was surprised as for the first time he had call in the day time. I answered and greeted him.

I am sorry to call you in your office time. I have sent you an email, want you to read it before we talk in the evening. He said and disconnected.

Strange, I murmured and returned to my seat. He wrote:

Hey Pri. You know I could not sleep all night yesterday fearing what will happen if you say no after meeting me. I have already discussed about you with my close friends, gave a hint to my elder sister even. I have started dreaming about you living in my home as my wife. Please tell me, on what all bases you can reject me. I am so restless thinking all this. Getting a song in my mind for my situation. It is from the movie Anurodh and the song is "Mere dil ne tadap ke". I am sure you will not be having this in your playlist as it is an old song so here are the lyrics. Take care

"Mere dil ne tadap ke jab naam tera pukara, kahaan se na jane chala aaya ye mausam pyara-pyara, mere dil ne tadap ke....

Tere raste pe main ankhein bichhaye baitha hun, tere intezar ki main duniya sajaye baitha hun.

Dekhein teri nazro ko bhaye na bhaye ye nazara. Mere dil ne...

Tera-mera pyar ik raaz hi rehta to achchha tha, soz na banta ye saaz hi rehta toh achchha tha.

Jane kya hoga jab hoga ye Milan hamara. Mere dil ne...

Dhadak raha hai dil, dil ko main kaise samjhaun, tujhse milun ya mile bin yahaan se chala jaun.

Aisa na ho tu ye dil tode, zamana hase saara. Mere dil ne tadap ke jab naam tera pukara..."

I downloaded the song to hear it before I reply. All lines of the song touched my heart straight and I felt exactly what he would have felt while typing this email for me.

I replied – Rest assured, looks will not be the reason at any cost. I like you for who you have been to me till today. I like your honesty. You know Mansi & Bharti already calls you "Jiju" and I kind of like it. Good bye, talk to you later on the phone and yes, I guess "I love you too". Cya

Arjun could not believe on what I had just written in my email so he called at night to confirm it.

Hi, I am leaving tonight from here and will be on sailing for another 4-5 days, he said.

Ok, I replied.

So no phone calls for this period but emails can be shared. It's fine. Which country you are going to?

Ah, we are leaving for Philippines.

Nice.

So, are you ready with the plan? I have heard Delhi is famous for its food.

I don't need a plan for guiding you through my very own Delhi. We have enough of places to roam around, I said proudly.

That's cool. By the way I hope your parents won't mind if I stay at your home for 4 days.

What? Are you insane? You can't stay at my home. What would I tell them, who are you?

Calm down, I was just kidding. You find out some good hotel near to your residence so that you don't have to travel much to visit me.

I will check. By when you will be able to confirm me your travel dates?

I can't say now. See it all depends on our departure and arrival from the last port. You won't believe we sometimes get our ticket just one day prior to our travel and even on the day of travel as well.
Whatever, I will need to apply leaves for the time you are here and that I have to do in advance so that there are no chances for my senior to get an opportunity of barking at me, I said.

He replied, I will try to confirm that ASAP. By the way today I called for two reasons. First, to hear you of course and

48

second to confirm if you only wrote your last email as I found a very colourful line there.

Which line? I pretended as I don't remember what he was talking about.

That you love me too, his voice full of hope and excitement.

Well yes, I think that I have fallen for you too. But I still want us to meet before jumping on any conclusion.

That's enough for me; I am feeling more confident now. I can't wait to see you now.

Same here, come soon. Ok, I will go and sleep now.

Why do you sleep so early? It must be just 10 pm there.

Because I wake up early too, at around 5-6 am.

Why? I mean that's a crime to wake up so early.

I have a habit of it since my childhood when I used to do everything
except study in day time. To cover up the loss, I was forced to study early morning.

Ok. But why now? You leave for office at 8 so what do you do in those hours. Get fresh, make tea, do some exercise on my terrace or sometime just walk and feel the early morning breeze. Later serving tea to all for waking them up and then after a bath get ready for the office.

Impressive but it can never be my cup of tea. When I am at home I can't wake up before 11 am.

You know, you have almost everything that I never wanted in my-would be husband.

Yeah, I know. But I am trying to change and you know I have already reduced my cigarettes from 12 to 8.

Only 8, wow. You deserve applause, I said with sarcasm.

It will be zero soon. It takes time but I will do it.

I hope so. Ok I will leave now. Good night.

Good night, sleep peacefully, have sweet dreams and I love you.

I know, I said laughing and disconnected.

Days passed and we shared numbers of email meanwhile, trying to know every little thing about each other. It was then we discovered we were poles apart, very different in nature.

He was a hardcore non-vegetarian and I even hated egg. He loved alcohol and cigarette and if I had given a wish by a jinnee, I would have asked him to remove these two things from our planet. He loved winters and I didn't. He lived a very haphazard life and I was in a habit of keeping everything on its right place. I was very practical and rarely emotional, he was vice versa. I was short tempered and he was rarely high with anger. My favourite dish was Maggi and he wondered WHY. I loved Shahrukh and he loved making fun of him. I was against PDA and he loved it saying, why to think what others are thinking. Nothing was same in our choice except one thing that we both fell in love through internet.

6.

It was the month of October, my cousin from Punjab was getting married (son of my eldest maternal uncle) and we all were very excited. Tickets were booked in advance and we all were there 2 days prior to the wedding. I along with Nitin, one other cousin and my siblings took out time from the rituals that were being performed at home and went to visit the famous Golden Temple. We also visited "jaliyan walan baag". We were enjoying ourselves to the fullest and had a blast in the wedding. It was fun to be a part of the procession and dance like crazy drunkards, I and Nitin were famous for it. The venue of function was at a distance of 60 kms from my cousin's residence. It was over by 3 AM, so we all came back to his home and decided to rest for some time.

We woke up with the noise of 100 of people. The car that carried bride, bridegroom, his mother, father, brother and Kishan maama (my youngest maternal uncle who used to live us in our home) met with an accident and all are in hospital. We all were shocked. The house which was full of laughter and music a while ago was mourning in every corner of it. We waited restlessly to hear about them and prayed that nothing was serious. At around 12 noon, we saw the bride, bridegroom, his brother, mother and father coming back in a car. The father of bridegroom got a fracture in his left hand; rest all seemed fine with minor scratches.

My siblings and cousin started thanking god for their well being when I shouted "but where is Kishan maamu?" followed by a moment of lull. Nitin rushed after my cousin who had just witnessed his best day of life turning to the worst. Nitin came back with teary eyes and told us that Kishan maamu and the driver were serious and in ICU. We so badly wanted to be there with him at this moment but nobody was allowed to meet him as he was in no senses in ICU. We all came back to Delhi leaving my mother there as she could not leave her youngest brother struggling alone. Days passed and he did not improve and was still admitted in ICU. My mother came back after 15 days when my eldest maternal uncle promised her to take good care of Kishan maamu. In next 15 days he improved a bit and got shifted to normal ward.

Time flew, Arjun was scheduled to sign off from South Korea and reach Delhi on 22nd morning. In office I made excuse of falling sick and took leave for 3 days from 22nd to 24th. Arjun booked his flight to Mumbai for 25th December night. He had landed in mid night but for his wish of me picking him from the airport he waited for me at the airport whole night. I reached at around 8:30 at the airport. My heart was beating faster with every thought of getting the first sight of him. We had seen each other in pictures only. It was a chilly morning of Delhi's winter and everybody wore as many clothes as they could which was making it even harder to recognize their acquaintances in the crowd. A sudden commotion at a phone booth of the airport thrilled my body. He was there, waiting for his turn outside to call me. He looked at me and hundreds of butterfly started playing in my stomach. I waived a "Hi" to which he smiled and headed towards me. My heartbeat doubled. There was a moment of lull and then we hugged, formally though.

We spoke again only after taking the taxi and headed towards the hotel he was going to stay in. He broke the silence.

It's really cold here unlike Mumbai where you don't get to know when winter arrived and went back.

Yeah, Delhi is famous for its winters, I replied.

So, you lied to me.

For your kind information Mr. Tripathi, I don't lie.

Oh, I did not know you are the hips of Shakira, he joked.

Ha ha… Try harder next time, I threw sarcasm.

Ok, but you did lie to me. You said you don't look as good as your pictures.

I blushed and said. You lied too, you said you don't look as bad as your pictures, I continued the humour and we both laughed.

We reached Karol Bagh and he checked in. While he went to take a bath, I switched on the television. I was enjoying the music when he came out and started removing the towel and changing into his pants to which I could not respond and immediately closed my eyes and there he was laughing out loud holding his stomach. Oh My God! You are so cute.

We hugged again and after we ordered our breakfast, we sat on the corner of bed and started discussing our future. We got so comfortable with each other that it seemed as if we know each other since ages and it's not our first meeting.

He then took out a box from his luggage and gave it to me saying "please accept a small token of love from me". I opened it and found a new Apple ipod in it. I remembered in one of our casual talks I had shared with him that I am saving money for buying an ipod. I was amazed that how he remembered it despite of hearing it in our early talks only. He had also brought chocolates for me, Mansi & Bharti.

We spent 3-4 hours just holding hands and talking about how it all started. I was noticing him for what type of a guy he was but to my delight he never tried to come closer to me. We discussed about almost everything. He told me about his family members in details, I did same. We then left for Connaught place, where my office was located as we had to meet Mansi after her office hours. It was just 3 pm when we reached there and Mansi was to get free by 5. We spent some time in wandering through inner circle, Mc-donalds and central park. We then headed towards my office. On our way Arjun asked me why I hated drinking and smoking so much. I told him how we had experienced many embarrassing moments just because my dad was an alcoholic and this was the reason I hated it ever since I knew that alcohol was the root cause of most of our problems. He promised me that he is trying his best to quit smoking and has already stopped taking alcohol.

We waited for Mansi near adjacent building so that nobody from the office could see me. Mansi came and we left for "Ugrasen ki baoli", a monument close to our office. We spent some time there and took an auto for our home. Arjun came along to drop us, on the way back we showed him our adda, i.e. C4-E market and he insisted to have momos there about which he had heard a lot from me but never tasted it.

Our home was at walking distance of 10-15 minutes from there. We helped him getting an auto for his hotel and walked towards our home. Even before I could ask Mansi about him she spoke, isn't he funny? I nodded. I shared my day with her and she could see the happiness in my eyes. By the time I reached home, I got an SMS from him.

Hey Pri, thanks for the day, thanks for having trust on me

54

and thanks for everything. You are not only beautiful with your looks but with your heart too. I can sense the tough time you have gone through at many points of life. I promise to give you the life you have always dreamt of. I love you.

Thanks to you too. It will be one of the most memorable days of my life. See you tomorrow. I love you too, I replied.

This day went on flying and morning is taking hell lot of time to come. It is difficult to wait for morning; he sent another text in response.

Just this night, I will be there tomorrow. Be ready by 9, tomorrow your guide will take you to some famous places of Delhi. Good night.

This night is not good, the day was brilliant. By the way I am sure you are not going to sleep before 3 hours. I will call you at around 9:30. Stay free. He replied.

At night we spoke for more than an hour on phone and shared hundreds of messages before going to sleep. Next day I reached his hotel by 9 and there he was, half asleep while brushing his teeth. He came forward to hug me but I asked him to take his bath first. We decided to leave after breakfast. I ordered breakfast and he went for bath. By the time he got ready, his breakfast arrived. We hugged before leaving and I felt some commotion on my forehead. A gentle kiss planted by him that made me surrender in his muscular arms. We hugged even tighter and slipped with the moment. He held my face in his hands which moved slowly near my ears and caressing my hair. I leant into him, our breath was heavy and both of us could feel the warmth. We didn't realize when our lips met and eyes closed. We kissed, soft at first, passionate later. I feel short of words to explain that divine feeling. He kissed again on the forehead and we left.

I took him to Lal Qila first and then after having some snacks in Chandni Chawk, we went to Qutub Minar. He was very happy visiting these places so I asked.

It seems you like monuments.

Not exactly, it's like my idea of party and going out with friends had never been different. It was always in a bar or pub. I have never visited such monuments but these are really amazing. I liked it.

Ok. So what all cities you have visited so far in India?

Mumbai, Bihar and now Delhi too, he replied. As I told you, I have been to few countries while sailing but in India I have not visited any city apart from these three.

How boring. You know I visit at least two places in a year. We will plan something soon, you must accompany us.

Pleasure would be mine indeed, hope your friends won't mind my company.

They would love it.
We hired an auto and headed towards my home. The days with him were flying at the speed of bullet. With every single moment my belief got firmer that he is the one. On our way to home Arjun asked, why does your father drink so much?

I am not sure, he never talks when he is in senses but may be because of the stress. You know my father was a teacher in our village. His first child was a son, who died at the age of 3 due to some illness. After that my dad could not stay in village anymore and came to Delhi. He started working with Bajaj Auto Limited as an accountant and time made him one of the best employee and a sort of friend with his boss. My father was not one of those who keep on producing daughters for the sake of a son but the death of first child made him craving for it and that's the reason we are 4 sisters today. After me my brother was born and with that my father got his happiness back but it was too late to realize that it's damn difficult to bring up 5 kids in today's era. He worked hard day and night and brought all of us to Delhi and here we started our education. May be the education of 5 kids, accommodation arrangement and marriage of all made him alcoholic. Anyways, leave it. It only spoils my mood.

I am sorry, he said wiping off the tears which were rolling through my cheeks.

It's ok, you know my father now owns this big house in Delhi, gave good education to all five of us and now has married all my three elder sisters without the help of anyone but after his retirement we were left with nothing that he had to take some loan for my brother's education that he is still paying off. That is why I am saving for my own marriage, I really don't want to burden him with anything again, be it my marriage also.

That's so very of you, my Priyanka.

I smiled while he spoke again. It hurts to see you sad but we need to discuss all this as your mother has already got indulged in that Australia-match for you. Suppose if your parents don't agree for our relationship, what will you do?

Well my father keeps on asking me if I have someone in my heart so that they can meet his family but that's always when he is drunk. So I think they will accept our relationship.

My question remains same, what if they don't? He asked maintaining the expression on his face.

I would go with their decision, I replied looking down.

He just said "ok" in reply, not knowing what to say but clearly looking heart-broken.

What? What do you expect? I asked raising my eyebrows.

Being honest, I would like you to go against them if they don't agree for our relationship, he replied earnestly.

Don't you dare to say that again. You have just entered in my life and they are the one who gave me this life that I am living happily today, I fumed.

See you are taking me wrong. We will of course try our level best to convince our parents but if still they are not ready for some illogical rituals, I don't want us to separate, he said in a requesting tone.

I can't promise anything over it Arjun. Only option we have is to convince them all, be it your family or mine.

But this is really not fair. Did you ask them before falling in love? Did you take their permission before saying yes to me? Why now then when we have already started dreaming a life together? He said reasoning and almost on the verge of getting tears.

Ok-ok, don't get upset. We will find out something. If we are meant to be together we will be. I tried to calm him down.

We slept discussing all ifs and buts through texts that night.
Next day again went on with roaming around the city. It was
25th December, Saturday and a full working day for me and
Mansi despite of being Christmas day (We were not given
any Indian holidays as we were serving the Russian
Embassy) I was on leave since last three days, so I planned
to attend office that day and Mansi and Bharti planned to
take Arjun on the tour. Arjun was upset and so was I but it
was his plan to spend first three days with me only. I
promised him to see him as soon as possible in the evening
and to drop him to the airport. They decided to go to
Adventure Island (an amusement park in Rohini). Everytime
I called to ask their whereabouts Bharti never missed an
opportunity to tease me by saying "arey yar, tu bar bar
disturb mat kar, we three are having so much fun here".

I so hated the fact that we were working that day and was
cursing the Russians when I received an SMS from Arjun.

"Tu jo nahi hai to kuch bhi nahi hai, ye maana ke mehfil
jawaan hai haseen hai"

I loved him for his musical romance and could not restrain
myself from making an excuse again in the office that I am
feeling dizzy for I had just got up from a three days bed rest
and left office at 4 pm. I reached Adventure Island by 5 and
called them to inform that I have reached. As it required a
ticket to enter there I waited in the mall outside. Arjun
stepped out first and there it was a huge, ear to ear smile on
his face as he spotted me.

I hugged them all and then came Bharti asking how come
you are here so soon, you were to leave office at 5?

I pulled her cheeks and said "Arjun told me how much you guys are missing me so I could not stay in the office anymore and rushed to meet you".

We spent some time in pizza hut, they showed me the pics they had taken in the amusement park and shared how they enjoyed every ride. I was so damn jealous but happy that they liked Arjun. We dropped Mansi and Bharti at Karol Bagh metro station and left for the hotel of Arjun from where we had to take his luggage. I had already booked a cab for airport, it came on time.

We were holding hands while seated silently in the cab, both afraid of leaving each other. I broke the ice and spoke, we should be happy that none of us changed our mind even after meeting personally. He smiled and landed his head on my shoulders and said.

You know there was a time, I had decided that I will never fall in love as I had seen a very disturbing love life of my brother. It was not disturbing for him only, my whole family has suffered because of it. This is the reason I always made it very clear to my girlfriends in past to not expect any commitment from me and those girls were of that type only. They were happy with a no-commitment relationship. Now I know how it feels to be in love, it's like being on the seventh sky. Never leave me baby, I would do anything to keep you happy and content.

Same here baby, you know after my break up I too had decided the same but Bhaggu had something else in his mind for us. For a change I can thank him once more.

I love you, he said planting a kiss on my forehead.

I love you equally, I said kissing his hands that held mine in it.

We reached airport. It was time to bid adieu to each other and continue with the long distance relationship and crave for the next meeting. We hugged for long and kissed when it was high time for him to leave. He promised to come back soon and left.

On my way back to home, everything played on my mind from the day we shared our first hello on facebook. It was tough to believe that it was all happening in real. He landed in Mumbai at 11 pm and sent me an SMS instantly.

"I am sure you must have followed your early-to-bed policy and slept by now. I am sending this message to say that I have landed safely and will be in home in an hour and that I am already missing you a lot baby. Sleep well, talk to you tomorrow. Love you."

He was right, I read his message in morning and replied.

"You have started knowing me well, just read your message. Love you and missing you too". Call me when you are free.

It was Sunday, so I called Mansi & Bharti to my home for a softdrink and maggi party. It was hard for Mansi to leave home on Sunday but she managed as Bharti went to her home to help her coming out and then they came over to my place. I asked them about Arjun, especially to Bharti as Mansi had met him once in the evening.

Give me the chocolates first that he has given to you for us, then only you can get my feedback, she said giving a wicked smile.

I gave them their packets of chocolate and before I could have repeated my question, Mansi spoke. He is nice yar, I liked him very much. What a physic he has, you are lucky to have got him. (Mansi had always been so slim that she always craved for a muscular man around her who can protect her in need)

Bharti said, I liked him for his sense of humour and how he feels for you. It is in his eyes that he loves you truly.

I blushed.

We fixed 9:30 – 10:30 for our telephone talks. In the day time we shared non-stop messages and waited all day long for the night to come so that we can speak on phone. Our love was soaring over the sky.

7.

It was 30th December. I was passing time watching some comedy show in the drawing room when my father called me in his room. As always he was fixed on his seat and drinking. I asked what does he want and why he had called me there. He started with asking about my health as he frequently did after getting drunk. He asked me to sit near to him which I followed getting irritated as the smell of whisky was getting on my nerves. He then Said:

You are not my daughter, you are my son. I am sorry for not doing anything today. You are my favourite kid among all who made me proud of being a father. You are the one who is running this family since I retired. You have done so much for us and look at me, I could not even save enough for your marriage. I could not do much for you my baby, I am so sorry. Please forgive me, he said started crying.

It made me cry too which brought the attention of my mother and she entered in the room saying:

"Tumhara naatak fir chaalu ho gaya? Wo office se thak ke aayi hai and tum ho ke usey rula rahe ho"

My father interrupted, you get lost out of the room. I am talking to my daughter and continued crying. I wiped his tears saying you have done a lot papa; you have made me what I am today. You are the one who have made me capable of doing all this which is making you proud today. Be proud of yourself.

He then came to his favourite topic, i.e. my marriage. I will get you marry the best man my daughter and tell me if you like someone, I will get you marry him. I found it a good opportunity to speak about Arjun and I spoke.

Papa, there is a guy. He is a good friend of mine and wants to marry me.

My mother got shocked as she discussed that Australia proposal recently with me and that time I did not say anything about it. She asked, what is his name?

Arjun Tripathi, I replied.

Thank god, he is Brahmin. "Kahaan se hai"?

His roots are from Bihar but he is settled in Mumbai with his family since childhood, I replied. My family, including my mother had a special disliking feeling for people of Bihar & Punjab. She got worried. My father then spoke.
No problem beta, you ask him to come and meet us. If the guy is fine and his intentions are pure, I will talk to his parents.
I could not believe my ears and was so happy. My mother was still quite. I then told her, mummy trust me he is a nice guy. He is educated, comes from a respected family, earns good and has recently bought a flat in Mumbai of his own. What else do you need?

"Wo sab theek hai but mann nahi manta, wo log humse bahut alag culture ke hote hain" my mother said.

Ok, you meet him once and if you will give me one reason for why I should not marry him, I will follow you. Now smile please.
She nodded and I hugged them both. I was on top of the world and waited restlessly for Arjun's call. I could not believe everything was going so smooth. I wished Bhaggu

was too busy somewhere to notice my happiness. I called Mansi & Bharti and shared with them what had just happened. They both replied with three words "party kab hai?"

I was talking to Mansi when Arjun called; I disconnected her call to answer his. Hi baby, he said affectionately. I repeated the entire discussion that I just had with my parents. He was super happy for his work of convincing my parents was half done. We congratulated each other and went on discussing our future. It was 31st next day, last day of the year & my brother's birthday. When I and my sisters were kids we missed to celebrate the birthday of four of us to celebrate our one and only brother's birthday with a bang. We invited all our close relatives from all over Delhi on this day. Since my father had retired our rare relatives came to visit us. So we were left with few of my cousins and my married sisters with the kids celebrating this day with us.

I was in mixed emotions that day, happy for what happened last night and scared for what will be the reaction of my sisters. My sisters reached our home with kids in the morning only. I got busy with the kids as I was the one they loved most and the one they feared most. I took them to nearby confectionery in the return of which they were supposed to wash my scooty. As soon as I reached home kids rushed into the bathroom looking for bucket, swab and a mug to start up their work. I heard some talks when I stepped the stairs, it was about me. I quietly listened to them and understood that my sisters were not in favour of my relationship with Arjun. I kept standing there to listen more but got distracted when someone patted on my shoulders, it was Nitin, famous as Neeru. He was my cousin cum best friend cum advisor cum everything. He was the son of my youngest Mausi (mother's sister). His father expired when he was just few years old, his uncle took his responsibility and loved him as his own son. He was much more mature than the guys of his age, fair, tall and very good looking.

What are you doing here? He asked.

I held his hand and took him to terrace directly and shared everything about Arjun, my conversation of last night with mom-dad and the negative discussion that was going downstairs.
Calm down, you just tell me one thing. Ladka sahi hai na? Haan, wo bahut achchha hai, I replied.

That's all. Nothing else matters. Ask him to come here once and meet our family. I will handle everything here.

I hugged him and we then went to face my sisters. My elder sister (Priya) was speaking, rather asking my mother when we reached there.

Do you have any acquaintance in Mumbai or in Bihar? How will you get to know about his family and the brood?

What do we have to do with whole brood? The families can meet in either city. I spoke.

Oh really, do you have any idea what their culture in Bihar is all about? They speak of dowry only in whole marriage talks.

Arjun is different, he is against dowry. I said firmly.

What about his family? Don't they expect anything from their son's marriage?

They will not have any problem with it.

Arjun must have told you this, right?

Yes, I replied.

See, we too have been through your age and trust me initially everything seems so rosy that you don't get to see the future clearly.

His parents may get ready initially but with the time they will taunt you for not bringing anything.

They won't and god forbids if they do, Arjun will handle it.

Their culture is totally different; you will die managing between
them and your desires. Priya di warned me again.
I made a wailing face.

Who all are there in his family? What does he do and how much he earns? Nitin tried to change the topic.

His father has retired recently from Indian navy, mother is a home-maker, elder sister is married, second sister is about to get married, then a brother and then Arjun. Arjun is in merchant navy and earns a 6 digit salary per month. He is even to get the promotion and after that he will be getting double of his salary.

Did you bother to ask him, if he really earns this good and settled well in Mumbai, why did he choose you from far away a city? Are not there girls in Mumbai? Priya di asked again.

I don't need to ask this, I know this is because he loves me.

67

Don't give me this love-shove shit, she fumed.

Then spoke my second sister (Nisha Di) "Na bihar mein hamara koi pehchan wala, na Mumbai mein koi. Kal ko kaat ke fenk denge dahej ki wajah se kahin, pata bhi nahi chalega"

Arjun is not like that. You at least meet him once and then give me a reason for why I should not marry him, I pleaded.

The reason here is that he is from a different community and I don't want any argument after this, Priya di said with anger and switched on the TV.

Nitin then tried to convince my mother. See mausi, community should not be an excuse, what I have heard about him, he seems to be a nice guy. Let's meet him once and then we will decide. We all know Pari (my nick name), she will never go against us.

Nisha Di then threw a taunt "if caste is not a problem then what happened when we chose a guy from different community"

We don't want to meet him and if he will come, tell him to stay prepared for insults. Priya di said and left the room, Nisha Di followed her. My mum turned towards Nitin and left saying: "I need to keep everyone happy and I am the one who is always mistaken."
That was my brother's first birthday that I did not enjoy. I called Arjun to share this with him. He answered.

You have long life, I was about to call you.

May be but seems our love life is not long for us to be together.

What do you mean? All ok? He asked nervously.

I shared everything that happened. He then laughed "arey itni si baat, maine kaha tha na main sab sambhaal lunga". You just leave it on me; I will handle both the families.

I felt better after talking to him. He then took my permission for drinking at New Year party as he was celebrating New Year with his friends after a long time. Since last many years he was sailing in the month of December.

For the night I allowed him. He promised that he will be in limits.

It was 1st January and everything was back to normal. Everyone was busy in calling people and wishing Happy New Year. I did not feel like doing so but then decided to change the mood so that my mood does not bring back their bad mood. I called Mansi and Bharti and we planned to meet in the evening. I also called few of my other friends. Arjun called me in the afternoon and told me that he was so drunk yesterday that he told his brother everything about me yesterday and also that my family is against it even before meeting him.

What the hell? Why did you drink so much? I asked furiously.

You are bothered about drinking? You won't believe what I did last night.

What more now? I fumed.

My brother was in the same party last night and I told him

69

everything about us. I hugged him tight and cried like a kid saying "I can't live without her and mujhe us hi se shaadi karna hai". He even hugged me back and said "you will marry her only, I am with you". You know me and my brother rarely talks as at times he drinks a lot which annoy me like nothing else. I am so embarrassed for how to face him now.

"Hmm" was all I had for reply.

Seems you did not get my point. If my brother is in my side, no one else in the family can go against my decision. So, problem from my family is solved.

Yeah, and it seems the problem in my family has just now arrived.

I will try my level best for convincing your parents.

You better do, as I will never go against my family's wish.

I know, you Lady-Shravan, he flunged.

After talking to him, I continued playing with kids. I pretended as if nothing happened yesterday and my family reciprocated the same way. My condition was similar to the duck that looks calm & smooth on the top of water but under that there is restless paddling.

On 2nd January my cousin from Punjab was coming with Kishan maamu who improved only a little in last 2 months. He was too weak to do anything else from going to bathroom. His wife (my maami) came from village to take care of him. Every time I saw him I could not stop my tears from flowing out. He was too changed to recognize at first glance, he was in his forties but it looked as if he was above sixty.

While he was on complete bed rest maami gave her everything in his care and he started improving day by day. We were happy seeing that. I started coming home on time and entertaining him sitting next to him on his bed. He could not laugh out loud like he used to do before, mostly on his own jokes but he tried to smile. Seeing him struggling to smile just a little always brought tears in my eyes.

Everyone at home was going through the same phase and my mother had tears in her eyes most of the time. I was so damn helpless that I could not even cry as seeing me cry everyone would have done the same. I shared my grief with Arjun and Mansi daily. I literally cried on phone many times while telling Arjun about our old good days with Kishan maamu.

Arjun again came to Delhi in January and stayed for 2 days. With every passing day I was getting to know him better and he was proving himself to be the best choice of mine. Arjun was an ideal son, an ideal brother and an ideal friend too. His best trait was his sense of Humour. I had merely laughed since Kishan maamu had come but he made me do that in just one minute of his arrival. We spent those two days in the company of just two of us. He came to pick me early in the morning and dropped me back late evening. He had lied at home that he was going to a nearby place with his friends and that's why he could not plan for more days but he promised to come back in next month.

On 26th January, it was just me, my dad, my brother, Kishan maamu and maami was at home. My mother had gone to her village to see my maternal grandmother as she was so ill that she could die any moment. She didn't want to go leaving maamu behind but maami assured her to take care of him. In the evening, I was sitting near maamu and reading newspaper for him while he was as always laying on his bed, dad was on his seat as always talking to his invisible friends who appeared after few drinks. Maami was busy in kitchen and Kamal (my brother) was with his friends in our street. Maamu tried to say something which I could not understand so I called maami. Maami also could not understand what he was trying to say as his words were not clear at all. We covered him with one more blanket thinking he might be feeling cold but he continued trying to speak to us.

I called my dad, brother, a neighbour and one of our tenants to see what is happening to maamu. I started rubbing maamu's feet and maami rubbed his hands. He got a bit better and suddenly fell silent. Maami said "lagta hai so gaye." My dad left the room saying in low voice "so gaya hai lekin hamesha ke liye". Hearing this I started rubbing his feet even faster, maami jiggled him to wake him up but nothing happened. I bursted with shrill cry and maami fainted. I was asked to inform my sisters. I called my sisters and cried like a kid as I said "didi maamu.........."

Both of them understood my unsaid words and rushed to our home immediately. My home was mournful once again. I was crying in solitude when Arjun called. I was not in a mood to talk to him but as they say "Best friends are those who hold your hands even tighter when you say – please leave me alone." So was he. I texted him not in a mood to talk, I will call you later. He did not stop digging me through messages like what happened, you are ok, etc until I gave up and told him everything. He consoled me and immediately booked his flight for next week. He even asked his mother to speak to my mother and console her. Arjun's mother called my mother to pass her condolence; she had a clear Bhojpuri accent and was very soft spoken.

Days were crawling. It was another Sunday and all my sisters were present when my mother was telling them that she got a call from Arjun's mother. She also said "baat karne se toh seedhe saade log lag rahe the." Nitin did not let those words fall and said "wahi to bola maine bhi, ek bar ladke se milne mein kya buraai hai." Nobody said anything in reply but I and Nitin had understood that the arrow has hit the target.

8.

Arjun came in February but as people at my home was still mournful, he did not find it a right time to meet them, I agreed. My monthly two-three leaves were fixed since I had met Arjun. We hated the fact that every day is followed by a night as we could spend only day time with each other and I had to reach my home by 9 pm leaving Arjun alone. It was his last day in Delhi when he asked me to plan something for an outstation trip with my friends so that he can be with me day and night for 2-3 days at least. I too found it a great idea. I asked Mansi, Bharti, Rakesh & Kapil and they all had their own reasons for saying "No". I was talking to Arjun on phone. He said "baby plan for some hill stations as I have never been to any hill station of India", I felt bad for him but told him that all my best friends are busy and are not ready to go.

That's sad but at least we two can go, he said casually.

That's not possible. How can just two of us go for night stay? I hesitated.

Why not? What is the big deal?

I will not be comfortable, I replied jittering.

Say in simple words that you don't trust me.

He seemed to be clearly annoyed with his words. I did trust him but something restrained me from saying yes. I tried to change the topic.

Oh come on, we will plan soon. My friends are busy in March; we can plan something for April.

I have my chief mate's exam in April; I won't be even getting time to come to Delhi in April, he replied a little frustrated.

Ok, so we will go in May.

Don't worry, now I will not join you for any outstation trip. You and your friends enjoy.

Don't over react Arjun.

I am over reacting? Did not you mean that you still don't trust me?

Where the hell this trust thing came from now?

It came from what you just said. Can you please elaborate why just two of us can't go for an overnight trip?

Well my parents won't allow if I tell them I am going alone with you. I made an excuse.

So every day that you take an off from your office and come to meet me, do you inform your family that you are not going to office and will be spending your entire day with me? He enquired with irritation.

I got his point and decided to tell him clearly that I am just not comfortable in spending a night with him.

He was speechless for a moment and then bursted.

That's the point. Now also say clearly that you still don't trust me enough. For your kind information Ms. Priyanka Pandey, the thing that can happen at night, can also happen at day time. Don't forget we have spent hours in my hotel room alone. Did I ever try to do anything against your will? Did I ever cross my limits? Mind you if I was looking for such things only, I would have got affairs in Mumbai so that I could spend as much time as I want instead of this long distance relationship where I hardly get to see you for two-three days in a month.

He was hurt and I knew I was the sole cause of it.

I am sorry Arjun, I did not mean that. It's just that so far I have gone for outstation trips with my friend groups only so got bit conscious about it. Let me plan something. Now don't do that just to please me.

I am not doing that to please you but to please me as I love visiting new places.

He apologized for shouting on me and I started planning the trip. I told my parents that I am going to Chandigarh for some official purpose. I could not say that it is a personal trip as Mansi and Bharti were not accompanying me. My mom knew that on all personal trips I take both of them or at least one of them with me. We were going to Jaipur, just me and him. It was Friday; Arjun reached Delhi in the afternoon and picked me from the office at 5 pm. We had our train in the night for Jaipur. We had our dinner in a restaurant near railway station. We spent the full night of travel in talking to each other.

You know the first time I came to see you; I was carrying pepper spray in my bag. I confessed.

Really? But why? He asked laughing.

76

I knew that we would be spending some time in your hotel and we were meeting for the first time so just for being on safer side I had kept it.

Oh my god! I can't believe it. So are you carrying it now also? I am just asking for this is your first night out with me.

No. I don't feel the need of it anymore with you. I said holding his arms tight.

He planted a kiss on my forehead and I rested my head on his shoulder.

Love was in the air. We reached Jaipur early morning. We were so tired that we dropped our plan of going out to see the city in the morning. We decided to freshen up first and after taking some rest in the hotel to move out for some sightseeing. We took our bath one by one. I was drying my hair when Arjun started pulling my leg.

OMG! We have just one bed here. Please don't spray that pepper stuff on me, please. I beg you.

Ok, if you insist, I won't.

We laughed and lied on bed cuddling and kissing. We slept and woke up at 1 pm. Arjun spoke to the receptionist and got a cab booked for sightseeing. We moved after our lunch. The cab driver was too talkative, he told us almost everything about Jaipur like why it is famous as pink city, the story behind "hawa-mahal" and "jal-mahal". We had the evening only for that day, so we could visit only the market as I had to buy something and "hawa-mahal" as it was near to our hotel. We then had our dinner at a good restaurant in the main market and went back to the hotel for night stay. We booked the same cab for next day's sightseeing.

None of us was sleepy that night as we had slept in morning only. So we talked about our childhood. I was a tom boy throughout my school days. I was as naughty in front of my parents as I was behind their backs. I always had a group of friends standing behind me considering me their group leader. On the other hand Arjun was quiet at home but naughty with friends. For rest of the things we were totally opposite to each other. We slept sharing our crushes and affairs that we had before meeting each other.

Next day we went to visit "jal-mahal" and other tourist places. We even enjoyed camel ride near "jal-mahal". We were back in the hotel by evening and had our dinner in our room only. We both were tired as we visited many places during the day and had to wake up early next day to catch our return train. We were cuddling in the bed.
I want this night to last forever.

I don't want morning to come. Arjun said hugging me tight.

Same here, I feel so complete with you. I replied.
I will talk to your parents soon. I hope they understand what I have to say.

But you were confident that you will convince them.

I still am but I am sure about what I have to say, I am sure of my feelings for you but I am not sure how your parents will take my words. I can just pray to God.

Huh, I can't even pray. Bhaggu loves denying my wishes.

It's not like that. There will be one day when you will admit that there is God.

I say that today also. I know there is God. I don't deny his presence. I am not sure of his form but yes he is certainly there. What I say about him is that I hate him to the core.

But why do you hate him so much?

There are many reasons for it but how it started is a secret and some secrets are better left secret.

I won't force you but will wait for the day when you will share this secret with me.

We smiled and kept an alarm for the morning. We reached Delhi in late afternoon. We met Mansi & Bharti in a mall near to our residence as Arjun was still left with some time for his flight. Mansi & Bharti were dying to talk naughty to me but could not do so in Arjun's presence. We bid adieu to Arjun from there only as I too had to reach home on time after a 2 days night out. As soon as Arjun took auto and left both of them caught me from both sides and started throwing their questions.

"Kaisa raha trip? Kya kya kiya? Kuch hua ya nahi? Kisne shuru kiya?" blah blah blah....

Both were disappointed to know that nothing like their imagination has happened. Bharti then said "strong of a guy he is to restrain himself even after being alone with a sexy girl like you for 2 nights". It made my love grow at double speed for him. For a fact that I hid from him, I was carrying my pepper spray there too.

Arjun was on the rank of second officer in merchant navy

and was preparing for the next rank for which he was to give exams in April. We did not meet in April and it was difficult for both of us. Arjun had promised to meet my parents in his next trip to Delhi. His exams were over and none of them went well which was quite obvious as I hardly heard him saying "I am studying". At many times I had to remind him that his exams are approaching in a reply to his numerous text messages.

May month started. I told my parents that Arjun is coming in few days to meet them. My mother shared this with my sisters who straight away denied coming to meet him as they were no way in favour of this relationship. I was heartbroken which was fixed by Nitin once again. He asked me to call Arjun to meet my parents for the decision of my parents is above the view of my married sisters. He also somehow convinced my sisters to meet him and then give their feedback. This time my third sister from Pilani (Rajasthan) also had come as it was summer vacation of kids. As the day of Arjun's arrival was approaching, he started getting nervous. He reached Delhi one day prior to the meeting fixed at my home. We met in evening after office and I told him about the nature of my family members individually.

It was hard for both of us to sleep that night. I sent Nitin at metro station to pick Arjun in the morning. I had asked Arjun to come clean shave but he could not find a salon near his hotel so he asked Nitin to take him to a salon first. He spent good time with Nitin and with his frank nature Arjun gained a little confidence. To my surprise my sisters were behaving much better now. They were preparing nice lunch, arranged snacks for tea and even made a sweet dish. I was happy and prayed that everything falls in place.

Finally Arjun entered with Nitin. He touched the feet of my

80

parents and elder sisters and shook his hands with Kamal. He had brought sweets and chocolates for kids. My mother greeted him well. I went to kitchen to check if my sisters are planning any prank. My second sister who was always attracted by the looks of people dragged me in the kitchen and said

Nice physic but is not he very dark?

I am also not fair and I like him the way he is, I replied.

My father had already taken his seat in his room for his afternoon session. My mother went twice to warn him not to drink much as Arjun was here. He as always did not reply and continued with his drinks. My sisters brought tea and snacks and took their seats. The drawing room was full with all interrogative eyes. On top of that my mother had called her cousin sister and her son also to give their views. Fortunately my cousin Mausi was cool and quite modern in comparison to my mother and so was her son (my cousin). Arjun was visibly nervous when I looked at him. I flew a kiss to make him smile. I signalled Nitin and he started the conversation which was continued by all.

Pari told us that you are in navy, said Nitin.

Navy alone is used for Indian navy usually and I am in merchant navy.

Ok. So how did you guys meet? Nitin asked further.

We met through facebook first, then emails and phone calls and then personally in Delhi.

So, does your family know about your relationship with Pari?

Priya Di asked in an interrogative voice.

Yes, everyone except my dad knows about her.

Why not dad? Nisha Di asked suspiciously.
My sister is crossing the marriageable age and we have not found a good match for her since last many years. Dad is always stressed with this so we cannot afford to tense him even more by saying that I want to get married.

So when do you actually plan to get married? Priya Di fired another question.

As soon as my sister gets married, Arjun replied in his usual calm voice.

I hope Pari has told you that we cannot afford dowry and till where I know your culture, dowry is the main thing in marriages of Bihar. What would you say on this?

Yes you are right. Dowry is the main thing in Bihar but we are living in Mumbai and I am not at all in favour of dowry system.
What about your parents? It was Deepti's turn to put her concern forward.

My parents have no issues with it because they know my capabilities.

My mother was very much relieved by now as her main fear was the dowry thing only. She then asked him. "You sail for 6 months in a year?"

No, aunty that was an old practice, now-a-days it's entirely up to us for how long we want to sail and when. I generally sail for 3-4 months.

See Arjun, you sure seem to be a nice guy but I hope you understand the differences of your and our culture too. Do you think your parents will be comfortable with Pari? Priya Di continued.

That's up to Pri. If she is ready to accept our culture, they won't mind teaching her anything and if she is not, nobody will force her to do anything. That is my promise to you.
Well said. Did she tell you that she doesn't know a single thing about cooking? Mom asked.

Achchha, then who makes the chapaati every day? I grinned sheepishly.

Yes aunty, she has honestly told me that she is good at making chapaati, maggi, tea and nothing else.

I gave him a I-will-see-you-later look. My Mausi defended me saying "so what? What else she has to do after marriage, taking care of kitchen and all. This is her age of staying away from kitchen. My cousin then started with his serious and important questions.

Will your father be ok with this marriage, asked my cousin?

Of course, he is not against love marriages. All he expects from us is to marry a Brahmin girl, he replied dutifully.

Where do you stay in Mumbai? Owned house or rented, he asked again?

Since my father has retired we have shifted to our own 2 BHK flat which I bought few years ago. Before that we were living in navy flats.

You have bought it means you alone or it has the contribution of your father and brother too?

I alone. My brother also booked a 2 BHK flat in Mumbai which is now under construction.

What is your education, asked Deepti.

Well, I joined merchant navy just after my 12th so you can say I am just 12th passed, he replied jokingly.

I screamed "OMG, kahaan main post graduate and kahaan ye 12th passed, rishta cancel" and all laughed. Arjun sent me a message escaping the eyes of all "everyone has asked at least one question and your dad is silent since I have entered. I hope he is not going to kick me out" to which I was about to reply but before that my father spoke.

You have bought this flat on loan?

Yes uncle.

What amount you pay monthly and how much you earn?

50k is the monthly instalment and I earn much more than that a month but that's only when I am on sailing. I don't get paid when I am at home.

Is it a permanent job?

Well it is not like land job uncle. It is a private sector but we don't have to work for one particular company, we can switch the company whenever we want.

See beta, you have already discussed almost everything with other family members. I won't ask any further questions but I want to say something which I want you to remember for a long time at least, if not lifelong.

Sure uncle, I am all ears.

I have five kids. Priyanka is after three daughters and my favourite among all. She was the most mischievous kid of mine until the age of 18 and I have seen her transforming from that to the most mature among all in just a few days and which makes me really proud of her. She started working just after I took retirement and also continued her studies. She has been earning alone for this home since then. She has seen a lavish childhood and has also experienced losing it all. Today I proudly say that I have a daughter like her who is not less than a son to me. There was a time when I had left no stone unturned for fulfilling my kids' desires and today I am struggling to fulfil the basic needs even. Today I have no savings, I even get threatened with the thought how will I arrange money for Priyanka's marriage? I feel helpless when I think of her marriage. It will be like something inside is dying. I won't be able to give you anything in dowry and to spend lavishly in her marriage. It will be a very simple function, may be in the temple with just few relatives around. So if you are saying that you are against dowry here and somewhere down expecting that things will be different at the time of wedding, you are wrong. We will let you down with your expectations in that case.

Uncle I have understood what you want to say. First of all trust me I am equally proud of your daughter. I promise I will take a very good care of your daughter and will try to give her everything that she desires and deserve. Secondly

85

please don't worry about the expenses of marriage because I and your daughter will take care of it. She is saving for her marriage and I promise your budget won't go beyond her savings even if it means we need to get married in a temple with no relatives around. Thirdly I am firm with my decision of no dowry. You know my salary now; do you think I need dowry to fulfil my needs? Uncle your daughter is one in a million and trust me I just need her in my life. I am deeply in love with your daughter and cannot imagine a life without her now. Please accept me and our relationship.

Everyone was silent when my mother said "chalo ab koi lunch bhi lagayega ya sab baatein hi karte rahenge". My sisters went in the kitchen to get the lunch when my niece came to me and said "Pari mausi mummy apko kitchen mein bula rahi hain". I was confident that Arjun has won everyone's heart so I entered kitchen smiling and asked "how is my choice?" to which Priya Di replied with a return smile "not bad". I was going back to the drawing room when Nisha di dragged me by my dupatta and asked rolling her eyes "if he is earning this much now, what he will get after his promotion?" I replied giving an ear to ear smile "double of it" and left. Arjun was looking for me only.

Where is the washroom? He asked.

Come, I will show you.
How is their reaction? Did your sisters say something in the kitchen?

Yeah, Priya di said you are pretty…..

What? Pretty? Don't you think nice, smart, dashing, interesting etc should be the compliment? Pretty is a compliment for girls not for boys. Anyways she gave one compliment at least.

Well I was going to say pretty ugly... She said you are pretty
ugly.
Really? He asked nervously.

I was kidding dumbo. She said you are nice and I am sure
everyone liked you. I will give you feedback of all later. I am
sure you are the hot topic for our today's late night gossips
session.

You are a devil. He said blowing a flying kiss.

Arjun had the flight back to Mumbai same day evening. So
we hurried up with the lunch. With the treatment Arjun was
getting by now, we both knew that we have done it. Kamal
called his friend with his car who lived in the next street to
drop Arjun to the airport. My cousin then came forward to
take the leave with Mausi and said to my mom.

Don't hesitate Mausi. Arjun seems to be a nice guy.
Yes but I am just afraid for what my relatives will say on he is
from Bihar, mom replied a little confused.
How many of those so called relatives visited you since Pari's
father retired? This caste and all is nothing Mausi. None of
these relatives are going to help you when god forbids your
daughter will ever be in any trouble after marriage, even if it
is arranged.
You are right but I will discuss with Pari's father and kids at
night and will decide then.

My Mausi then came forward and said hugging me tight
enough "mast choice hai, mujhe to ladka bahut pasand aaya"
I smiled and not to mention it was an ear to ear smile.
The result of the long discussion at night was that they were

all ok with this relationship but my mother wanted to speak to Arjun's mother first to ensure that his family also knows about it. Arjun arranged that too, he asked her mother to talk to my mom and she ensured my mother that the only reason for his father not being aware of our relationship fully is that at present he is worried about his daughter's marriage. My mother was satisfied and we were on cloud 9 as we did not need to hide anything from them. Arjun called at night and said "your father really loves you a lot".

You know Arjun, he has done a lot for us. Many of our relatives are in Delhi and their families are in village. They go to meet them once or twice a year, send some money every second month and their duty is done. My father worked hard for not falling in that category. He brought us all here and gave good education. He hardly talks to us but when he does, I can't tell you in words what feeling we get.
I understand. He was almost in tears when he was talking about you. I salute your maturity baby. Thanks for stepping in my life.
Thanks but you know if you had met me before 2007, you would have never said that.

Why? You started working in 2006, I am sure you were mature enough that time too.

No, I wasn't. Whatever I am today is just because of Puneet Sir.
Your senior in VFS Global, right. He had a sharp memory.

Yes, You know when I joined VFS Global; I was just a girl who was full of inferiority complex, full of hatred for dad for drinking this much, full of hatred for mom for always being biased for her son, full of hatred for Bhaggu for always doing opposite to my wish and need. You know I even was not willing to complete my graduation. I so wanted to quit it as I joined that with my best friend Babli who committed suicide just before four days of my birthday. You know, I was the last friend of hers whom she spoke to and I don't know the reason of her suicide. She didn't tell me she will be taking this step in an hour. I was just working for the sake of my family. It was not the career I wanted for me, it was so not the life I wanted to live.

I am so sorry to hear about Babli but how Puneet sir changed you as a person then?

You know I always had a bad habit of keeping my fears and tears to myself only, a bad habit that always gave me depression only. We did not like each other in our first meeting but gradually I realized he was not that bad. He was a senior to my senior but a person of simple living high thinking. So impressive with his talks that nobody would have ever asked him to stop when he speaks. We had our homes in the same direction so we accompanied each other on many occasion. On our way back to home we used to chat a lot. He asked me many times what I hide inside me and what the sorrow behind my naughty smile is. I took few days to open up and since then he is the one I don't hide anything from whom.

It sounds interesting, he said lovingly.

You remember I told you how my both elder sisters were involved in some affair when my dad decided to marry them soon and as he was not in favour of inter-caste marriages. Priya di was in first year of her graduation and quitted it. Nisha Di was never interested in studies so she did not even opted for graduation and got married before that. My third sister Deepti was the most decent among all and wanted to pursue higher education and go for a career. She was in second year of graduation when we had to marry her as my dad had met with an accident and was at a stage where doctor has asked us to stay strong for anything could have happened to him. My mother got frightened with the thought of marrying two daughters and a son alone after my dad so she fixed Deepti's marriage instantly. She had to drop her graduation because of this marriage and pregnancy later on. Puneet sir made me realize how my parents would feel when I will be completing my graduation as I will be the first one to graduate from my family despite of the fact that I am the youngest of four sisters.

Nice, kaafi door ki sochta tha banda.

Yes and he was quite right in everything he ever said to me. I was the first to graduate in my family and everyone in my family was so proud of me when they heard about it. He erased every poison that I had gulped. He removed the hatred I had kept within me for anyone in my family. He made me see the positive sides of everything around me. Today I get most compliments on my confidence and it is all because of him. Today people praise me for whatever I do for my family which is all because of him. He taught me how to survive in corporate world. He asked me to save at least something out of my each salary for my own marriage when I shared with him that my father has zero saving at present. In short, he is the reason behind this changed person whom you love today.

I would love to meet your sir, if he doesn't mind.

Sure, he too wants to meet you.

9.

We talked freely now and did not need to delete messages of each other for anyone could read it. Finally we were kind of feeling like an official couple and with that started the usual problems of every couple. Arjun was more confident now and started behaving as if we are already married. First thing after leaving Delhi he asked me to do was to change my relationship status on facebook which was against my nature as I never appreciated public display of affection.

Why do we have to advertise our relationship? I asked irritated.

It is because I don't want any tom, dick and harry to keep sending you messages with friendship proposal.

What's wrong if they do? I can simply say no to them.

What's wrong in changing the status? Are you still not sure about decision of marrying me?

You are impossible Arjun. I don't want to do it because I have many other relatives in my friend list and I don't want them all to spread the news until we get officially engaged.

What a non-sense excuse. You know I can't get officially engaged until we find a good match for my sister.

I know and I am not forcing you to do it. It's just that I am not comfortable in doing what you are….

I could not complete my sentence before he disconnected the call which made my anger transcend. I decided of avoiding him for at least two-three days to teach him a lesson but as I said he was that sort of a person who would never leave his beloved alone especially when she is in a bad mood.

He called me back in night. We started with casual talks, then with soft talks to solve the disputes, then with same arguments of morning and finally with hanging up with go-to-hell note.

Emotionally, I was much stronger than Arjun. I was feeling very restless inside but restrained to call or message him. He too tried his best but ended up in calling me in the evening again.

So, you can easily live without me? You don't feel anything if we talk or not, right?

Just say what you have to say and leave. I replied back furiously.

How can you stop talking to me for so long?

Because I am mature enough to understand that no one dies without someone.

True. Goodbye then.

He disconnected and I was too angry for why the hell he calls when he does not want to patch up things between us but felt bad as I then realized that I was very rude despite of the fact that it was him who called leaving his ego behind. I called him back and he didn't answer at first. I tried again and he answered saying "sorry baby, washroom gaya tha". I was shocked for he was talking as if nothing had happened between us. I replied back – It is ok.

Baby please don't fight, it hurts not talking to you.

Same here.

Ok, I will be honest. See I really get jealous when guys flirt with you every time you upload a new pic.

I know but most of them don't really mean what they say.

Trust me, many of your male friends will start ignoring you as soon as they know you are committed but that is good as such people can never be counted in true friends. These people are in your touch just because you are a good looking girl who is single as an add on.

Ok, I concede. Check Facebook after 30 minutes. Right now I am going to make chapaati.

Thank you. I love you.

I love you too.

I hung up and spent my kitchen time in thinking about all ifs and buts. While having my dinner I logged into Facebook and went to make the changes but ensured all my gossip lover relatives are blocked before changing the relationship status. I was just about to log off when received a notification. It was Arjun's comment on the update - Priyanka Pandey changed her relationship status from "single" to "in relationship with Arjun Tripathi". He made a kissing smiley on this update to which I made a simple smiling smiley.

It was just the starting of our taking-for-granted phase of our relationship. The Facebook whom we didn't mind thanking once for introducing us to each other was now the reason of most of our disputes. We had disputes on the friend requests I received on facebook. Arjun now had the problem of why I accept friend requests of any random guy which later turned to why I share my phone number with friends whom I just know of their existence through Facebook.

So what? I don't share my contact number with all. I give it to the people whom I find nice after knowing them for some time, I replied in anger.

Oh yeah and only through Facebook, you get to know if that person is of a good character or not?

Mostly, I replied getting even frustrated.

And what you do in cases they turn out to be a cheap guy just wanting to gel with random girls?

It has rarely happened. If they do, I block them.

My question to you is why have you to share your contact number with them in the first place.

Arjun don't you start interfering in my choice of friends now. I need not to ask you before making every new friend.I just don't want any guy to even get the opportunity of flirting with you.

You are being over possessive and it irritates me.

Everything I do these days irritates you. I am going to marry you and I have every single right of being possessive of you.

Fine. Discussion ends here.

I hung up. I kept wondering if it was the same guy I fell in love with. I thanked Bhaggu for bringing Pramod Bhatt in my life before I had Arjun. I met Pramod Bhatt through Facebook only and he proved out to be one sincere guy who can be counted as true friends. He was from the same community as mine and lived in Bangalore. I started avoiding friend requests from stranger guys and if ever added any, I restrained talking to them in chat. I was now habitual of talking to Arjun everyday so the day we fought and didn't talk to each other made me very restless. Both of us tried our best to not fight on small things but then it was Arjun always who had a problem with some or the other thing of mine. Next we fought on my office. Arjun used to come once in every month to meet me and I took leave every time he came. I even crossed the leaves specified in my employment contract for which I was getting negative remarks from my HR head. Arjun was planning his next trip for 4 days including Sunday when I asked him to make it for 3 days only as I will be able to take 2 days leaves to the maximum.

Now your job is more important than me? He started with his taunts again.

Why don't you talk straight Arjun? When did I say that now?

What else you mean then? I come spending thousand bucks just to meet you here and you can't take leave from your bloody office.

I have already told you how my HR have asked me to not take any further leave in next few months.

Tell him my fiancé will be out for sailing soon and I will not need any leaves for few months then but now I need leaves as I have to meet him.

You are not the only relation I have on this fucking planet. I may need leave when you are sailing for some family function or friends outing.

So, you mean outing with friends is more important than me?

I also mentioned family functions.

I know what you meant. By the way what will they do if you don't obey them and take leave? Deducting some amount from your salary? Who cares?

I care Mr. Arjun. I work for my family's living. I care for every single penny I earn. Mind you it is not just about getting some money deducted from my salary. I care about my reputation in the office. I don't want to get accosted for the same thing again and again.
Ok, next time he says something on taking leave. You quit the job. I will send you money equivalent to your salary.

Keep your money with you and don't ever dare to say that. Till the time we are not married don't ever try to stop me from earning the living for my family.

I didn't mean that. Ok I will come for 3 days only. Will let you know once I am done with the booking.

I kept thinking for long after disconnecting the call. I knew he wanted to spend time with me but I also knew how important it was for me to work. He could have easily afforded to take care of my expenses even if I didn't work but my self-respect never allowed me taking this step. He many times tried to get me some expensive things which I refused as I was afraid of people suspecting me for getting in this relationship for his money only. Arjun came and made things again normal between us. I could see it in his eyes how much he loved me. I convinced myself that the only reason for his possessiveness is his love. He was anyways right with one of his statement that most of my male friends are friends to me because I am single and they expect to fill it. It actually happened, ever since I had changed my status on Facebook and announced in public that I am committed, most of my male friends had eventually disappeared. We fought, we shouted, we got mad at each other but at the end we always made out as we loved each other truly.

Since he didn't clear his exams he had to set sail sooner than it would have been. He came to meet me few days before joining his ship. I cried hugging him tight at the airport when he was about to go back to Mumbai. He promised to stay in touch through emails and phone whenever possible.

I got busy with the work and impressing my seniors with minimum leaves in those 4 months. Arjun called almost every day even if it was just for 1 or 2 minutes. Distance brought us even closer. I waited desperately for him to come back and he waited to see me again. Time flew and he came back. We went to visit few other cities of India after his return. We even went out to places with my friend circle too. They all liked him as a person and appreciated my choice. Everything was going smooth between us except few small fights. Meanwhile my family kept asking me if they have found some match for Arjun's sister and I kept giving the same answer "They are trying".

Year passed and I was again offered a promotion by my boss. It was now the position of my senior whom I hated the most in entire office. My boss had caught him making money illegitimately. Everyone in office knew he was committing fraudulent activities but no one dared to say anything against him as no one had the proof either. Though everyone knew that with not a very handsome salary he had managed to own a flat, some land and a four wheeler which was quite a proof that it is not because of his salary only. Boss was planning to terminate him but did not say that clearly at first as he wanted him to work with us till the time I fully take over. I hesitated at first for I will be able to take that role or not as it was a different work all together. I discussed with Puneet sir and he scolded me for even taking time to think on it. He asked me to accept it at the earliest.

I accepted the promotion but to my bad luck I had to learn from the same guy I was going to replace. His job profile included handling our personal clients and coordination with the Embassy. He never taught anything heartedly but kept threatening me with his yokel like jokes. He one time even told me "Madam zara sambhal ke, aajkal log dushmani nikaalne ke liye, chehre par tezaab daal jate hain" followed by his uncouth laugh. I shared everything with Arjun and Puneet Sir. They boosted my confidence saying he is just trying to threaten you. Avoid him and give your best in new role. I faced many difficulties during that phase of learning as he many times gave me some task to perform as a test which he had never taught me how to do and on notifying that his answer was same always "Madam sikhaya to tha, aapko yad nahi hoga". Gradually I learned everything by noticing his style of working. Everyone was impressed as I was much more sincere and hardworking than him.

On realizing that boss is planning to terminate him, he himself resigned for escaping the humiliation of being terminated. I had got my other friend Tanya from childhood days appointed in my previous position. Mansi and Tanya were now working under my supervision. I worked hard and demanded a good hike in next increment. I started getting a better salary and recognition too as I was now the main face of "Russian Visa Department".

10.

Arjun tried to come every month to meet me and even made me fly to Mumbai the month he could not come. We now stayed together every time we met. At home, I sometime made excuses of official trip and sometime friends outing. We were enjoying this phase to the core and with every passing day Arjun kept proving his love to me. On the other hand my family was getting restless for we were taking a lot of time to take this relationship to the next level. One Sunday they all caught me finding a chance and started bombarding their doubts.

I hope you are still in mood of getting married to each other only, if not you can let us know. We will start finding another match for you, Priya Di started.

Of course we are.

May we all know but when? Relatives keep asking me when you are getting married, mom asked.

Mom please now you don't start. You talk to Arjun often and know how worried he and his family are for his elder sister's marriage.

It has been two years almost since we are listening the same excuse. What if she does not get married for next 4-5 years, Priya Di asked.

Don't be so rude. They can't get her married anywhere. It is just taking time. Why are we in a hurry?

It is because we are from girl's side. We are not looking for any match for you thinking you will marry him. I have even said no to the proposals that few relatives had brought for you giving them some lame excuses. What if some day, you come to us saying we have broken up?

I won't mom. We love each other and will marry for sure.

Every couple in their initial days say the same thing, Priya Di murmured.

The argument cum discussion went for long and left me with a headache. I discussed everything with Arjun at night. He promised to visit my family soon and talk to them. He did keep his promise and came to meet my family and convinced them that he and his family is really trying hard to get his sister married and once this is done, he will marry me at the earliest. Arjun had a charming convincing power with the help of which he calmed my family once again.

One day when I was busy with a lot of work around, my boss called me and assigned me a duty of finding a good guy for filling the post of my ex-senior who had already left the organization by now. After him, a Russian lady also left who was working with us as a translator as she got a better opportunity. I was over loaded with work as I was now taking care of the responsibilities of my ex-senior and ex-translator also. I was not translating the documents as my Russian was not that good but I was now burdened with her other jobs like attestation and legalization. I had too much work on me that sometimes I even shouted on Mansi and Tanya for some minor mistakes which they didn't take positively as they were friends to me before being my subordinates. On top of that Arjun and I were making new records of fighting every week. I was going through a rough time with too much job responsibilities, disputes with my best friends and souring relation with my love.

I wanted to bring some known person to work with me as I did not want to burden myself with unnecessary unhealthy competition. I contacted my old friend Rohan with whom I had worked in the visa centre of Australian High Commission. Fortunately he was looking for a better opportunity which he somehow managed to find in our company. He was a hard working and sincere guy. He took no time in learning all the things I taught him and sharing my burden equally. He was shy at first and when he opened up, he turned out to be a cute little monster for all the girls in office. He helped me equally in dealing with two major and complicated group travels. We worked hard for two months and got appreciated by all. As I was heading the Russian visa department already, Rohan was assigned the task of handling visa processing of other countries. I always knew that I will be leaving the city and shifting to Mumbai soon after marriage so I decided to train Rohan on Russia visa so that my boss brings no one after me from outside for my filling. I trained him on every small thing that I was doing in my job and he learnt everything at an amazing speed.

We were spending a lot of good time together in office and very shortly he was in the category of my best friends. He also started joining me in all the day-picnics that I planned with my friends. After I was relieved from those two hectic groups, I had planned a trip to Pondicherry with Mansi, Rakesh and Kapil. Rajneesh and Pramod were joining us in Bangalore as our flight was to and from Bangalore itself. Arjun had not joined us as in the last trip where I and he had gone to Rishikesh for river rafting with Mansi, Bharti, Rakesh, Rajneesh and Kapil, I had a little dispute with Rajneesh. He had issues with me that I was giving my maximum attention and time to Arjun instead of friends. Arjun did not want that to repeat so he did not join me even after asking him for number of times. I had noticed it many times that whatever plan I was making with my friends where Arjun is not involved was turning out to be a point to argument. For xyz reasons Arjun and I fought every time I went out with friends without him, be it just a movie, a day picnic or an outstation trip.

I was meeting Pramod and Rajneesh after years so just after meeting them we got busy in talking and discussing the further dc we do next. I thought of calling Arjun to inform that I have reached safely but then didn't call thinking he must have slept by now and it will not be good idea to disturb him at this moment. I had last spoken to him after taking my seat in the aircraft. We got into our cab as soon as we found our driver as we had to rush for Pondicherry directly from there. I was too sleepy and fell asleep just after taking a seat in the cab. Arjun called on phone and Rakesh picked it as I was sleeping. Rakesh told him that we have reached safely and just started with our journey to Pondicherry. Although I was sleeping, I heard him say "Arjun" and instantly woke up. Our first fight started with "why the hell I did not bother to inform him that I have reached" and it went on till I reached Delhi.

We were having a gala time with each other, roaming around the city, having food at almost every famous restaurant, dancing and singing in the guest room. I did take out maximum time to speak with Arjun as he was very possessive and did not leave a single chance to taunt me. Day by day he was getting worse with his choice of words he used for taunting. I pretended to smile in front of my friends and cried deep inside every time I was alone. It was my last night in Pondicherry and we all took a walk by the beach after dinner, when Arjun called.

Must be feeling bad for it is the last day there, he taunted.

Not really. I am kind of happy that going back to home.

So, how was the trip? You must have enjoyed a lot with your best friends (in a teasing tone).

Yes.

Read your status on Facebook which you posted the day before you left.... "Badtameeezi ek bimaari hai, jo dheere dheere budhaape mein badal jati hai... Main kehti hun jab tak budhapa nahi aata, thodi badtameezi hi kar lein..." I mean to ask badtameezi theek se ki ya nahi apne dosto ke sath.

You are the limit Arjun. I wonder why the hell I am still with you.
Even I don't feel any better baby.

Go to hell and don't you dare call me back, I disconnected the call in anger and cried out loud. Mansi came and hugged me tight. Arjun kept sending provoking messages to me, blaming me on everything to which I did not reply. I joined back in office. Arjun and I did not talk to each other for next few days. We always made up as we loved each other truly. We both were dying inside to talk to each other the way we used to do before. It was mostly him who initiated the talk after a fight and after every fight we found each other even more loving than before.

Soon Bharti was getting married in November to one of his colleague and Somya to his boyfriend in December. Bharti had told me everything about it in our early morning scooty rides on Sundays. Mansi and I were very excited for both the marriages, especially for Bharti's as we were much closer to her. Arjun was sailing so he could not enjoy these occasions with us. We enjoyed each and every function and custom of Bharti's marriage as it was first marriage in our group. Mansi was doing her teaching course from Indore and her exams were due in the month of December. As a result she could not attend Somya's marriage. The day before her marriage I got a bad backache and I too could not attend it.

With two of my close friends now married, I was being pressurized by my family for my marriage. I too started feeling bad now as we had already been in the relationship for two years now and yet there was no sign of his sister's marriage. One day Bharti had come to her home to visit her family and I was there to meet her. Her mother than caught me and asked.

When are you getting married now, beta?

Hopefully soon aunty, I said trying to ignore this topic.

Once people know about your relationship, you should get married ASAP beta. Time is very bad.

Yeah, we are just waiting for his sister to get married and we will marry soon after that.

In today's era how does it matter who is marrying before whom.

I kept quiet to stop the discussion but I was tired of giving this excuse to everyone who asked me about my marriage. 2013 was very tough with many such situations. People, especially relatives kept worrying about my marriage and irritating me with their questions and suggestions. Family kept pressurizing me to fix their meeting with Arjun's family which was not possible as they were still prioritized his sister's marriage. Every time I faced such situation, I took out my anger on Arjun over the phone and he like always calmed me with his maturity. I believed that it was no one's fault for the delay in my marriage as everyone had valid reasons, not of his sister for not getting married soon, not of his father who was worried about his daughter's marriage, not of my family who were worrying about their daughter's future and it was not the fault of mine even. I think the time or the intention of Bhaggu was not in my favour as always.

Every Saturday we were allowed to reach office at 10 instead of 9 as it was a non-working day for Russian Embassy. Mansi and I enjoyed those Saturday morning in different ways, like going to mc-Donald or some other restaurant for a nice breakfast, wandering through Connaught Place, spending time in central park or even enjoying a refreshing tea at a small tea-stall near our office building. Sometimes even Tanya and Rohan also joined us. Mansi also used to visit a kali-temple in Connaught Place on some Saturdays. I rarely accompanied her and whenever I did, I sat outside on a bench. Our Saturday-morning routine was about to change as Mansi was starting going to kali-temple every day for some 40 days worship system. I hated it as I was now habitual of travelling to office with Mansi. She started leaving at least 30 minutes before me to reach office on time after her temple visit. With work all day round I was rarely getting to talk to her in office too and then I found Rohan near me. We were working on the same line, I was teaching him everything that I was doing so got to spend maximum time of office with him.

With the changed designation, my office timings also got changed. From 9-5 it was now 10-6. I didn't want to travel alone in the morning so I would travel along with Mansi to reach office at 9 but in the evening I rarely got to leave my office before 5:30. After spending the whole day with Rohan, my topic of conversation with Arjun was a little different now as it included more of Rohan and less of Mansi. Arjun due to his over possessive nature did not take it positively. We started fighting on my plans with Rohan even if we were going with all my friends. We did not talk to each other for many days. I felt so lonely with Bharti not around, Arjun was sailing and always on fight mode, less time to spend with Mansi and rare friends around. I was cursing Bhaggu for bringing me in this relationship with Arjun and changing my life dramatically but then we got a ray of hope as his parents had found a guy for his sister.

11.

In no time it was all fixed and she was to get married in the month of July. Me and my family were all excited for I too will be getting married soon now. Arjun knew that he will not get time to visit me for some time now so he came to meet me few days before to her marriage, I helped him in shopping the items required in a marriage for which Delhi was much famous than Mumbai. I was not invited as the marriage was held in their native place and according to their customs "would-be-daughter-in-law" cannot enter in in-laws house before marriage. I did not mind as the happiness of her getting married was much more than the fact that I was not invited. Her marriage was one day prior to Arjun's birthday. We could not even talk properly on his birthday as he was busy with her farewell preparation. Arjun compensated it with a surprise visit on my birthday which was next month.

I started dreaming about my wedding dress and the life after marriage in Mumbai. Everything around seemed rosy to me and I was on the top of the world. However the dreams don't take much time to break. Arjun called next day:

Finally after so many days, I have slept properly. One north Indian marriage brings hell lot of work.

Yeah. I have experienced that in my 3 sister's marriages. All went fine?

Yes. You know she will be shifting to Delhi after one month as her husband works in Delhi.

Great. I will go to see her when she arrives here.

She would love to see you.

Arjun, when are we getting married now? My family is after my life since I have told them your sister's marriage is fixed.

Come on yar, my sister just got married. I need time to talk to my father about you.

"Hmm" was all I could say not wanting to spoil his mood.

Don't get sad now and I don't understand why do you worry so much? You seem to like deteriorating your health, just go and check your weight. You know, you have left zero figures far away.
I worry because my family is worried for me.

Baby you know my situation. We have already started looking for my brother's match and hopefully he will get married soon. We will marry soon after that.

What? Now from where your brother's marriage has come in between?

From where means what? He is elder to me.

But you never said that we will get married after your brother. How many more lies Arjun? You promised to quit smoking 3 years back and you are still trying to do that. You said you have quitted drinking and you still keep seeking permission for occasional parties which are very frequent. You promised that we will marry soon after your sister's marriage but now I have to wait for yet another marriage. I hate Bhaggu for bringing you in my life. I hate you, Arjun.

I said and disconnected the phone. He kept trying but I did

not answer. He then messaged me "I am sorry baby, I know I hurt you a lot but trust me it's never intentional and you are the one I love the most. Give me at least one chance to explain myself". I switched my phone off after reading the message. He then called on my mother's phone and after some formal talks; my mom gave her phone to me and I spoke in anger.

What?

Phone kyun off kiya
You don't have to tell me what to do and what not to.

Baby please. Can we talk and solve the misunderstanding?

My misunderstanding is all clear now. You do whatever you want to do and I will do what my parents want me to do.

Achchha baba, we will get married soon. I am coming in few days. Let's plan something as I want to spend all my time with you then.

I am really sleepy now. I will make the plan and talk to you tomorrow.

You are still angry with me? I know you are.

No I am not. Just not feeling like talking to anyone. Please Arjun, let's talk tomorrow.

Ok-ok. I will call you tomorrow. Now don't burden your little head and keep thinking negative. I love you and will do so forever.

I love you too. Cya

I hung up promising I won't think negative and will go to sleep now but I could not keep my promise and with all the negative thoughts in my mind, I caught a bad headache and fever next morning. I could not go to office next day and when Arjun got to know about it, he even fought on why I hurt myself with negative thoughts. Arjun booked his flight instantly and came to me, this made me realize he loves me much more than I love him. He spoke to me in front of my family about his brother's concern as I was lying on bed.

Baby, you know I have just given my exams and hoping to get the positive result. I will need to sail after the results with promotion at hand. All I was trying to explain you was by the time I will come after this sailing my brother's marriage must have got fixed. He is elder to me; secondly you know he has suffered a bad relationship in past and still trying to cope up. We all want him to get married first so that he does not start consuming more alcohol taking our relationship in negative way.

Fine. I understand everything what you want and mean to say. You just answer my one question. I waited for three years for your sister to get married. What if your brother takes another three years to get married? You want me to wait that long?

He won't take that long.

That's not the answer to my question Arjun. What if he does?

I will give him 6 months to get married, if he still does not take it seriously, we will get married.

111

Good. Your time starts now. Hopefully we are getting married in February or March then.

He nodded and I was satisfied. He left for Mumbai same day evening. He cleared his exams and got promoted as chief officer. His income got double and he joined ship soon. I kept writing to him and waited desperately for him to come back. His brother seemed in no mood of marrying in near future which remained a constant topic for mine and Arjun's arguments. I kept sharing with him how my family was constantly after my marriage as now his sister had got married which had been our sole excuse since last 3 years. Arjun tried to speak to his family from ship that he is getting pressure from girl's side (my family) but they kept ignoring him giving priority to his brother's marriage. One day when I was in office, my cousin Nitin called me.

Kahaan hai?

In office. What happened?

Meet me at Barakhamba metro station in the evening. We will go back in my car. Kuch zaroori baat karni hai tujhse.

Ok.
Nitin's office was in the same location as mine. From my family he was the strongest support to me. I was hoping he does not talk about Arjun in the evening as it was seriously not easy to explain anyone that now Arjun wants to wait for his brother's marriage. We met in evening and chatted on our way back.

You know Kamal loves a girl, he asked.

Yes I do and her name is Naina Joshi.

How do you know? He asked confused.

Facebook tells almost everything, I grinned.

Ok but you don't know what they are going through. They are in this relationship since last 4 years and love each other truly. She has one younger brother who is studying. Naina's grandfather is the one who has actually brought up these two. He is too old now and wishes to see Naina getting married before he dies. She is under too much pressure of parents for marriage.

Yeah, I didn't know this.

You know when Naina asked Kamal to come and talk to her parents, he simply denied saying "I cannot marry before my sister as she is elder to me". He even tried to talk to you to know when you are planning to marry but then I told him that Arjun will not marry before his sister. His sister was not married then. So he lost hope and told Naina, he can only talk to her parents when your marriage is fixed.

I was going through his profile few months back and felt that he is going through a break-up.

Break-up? She even got engaged to a guy selected by her parents, Nitin said in a sad tone.

Oh no, really? I asked in disbelief.
Don't worry. They have got second chance. That guy turned out to be a disgusting fellow and the engagement got dismissed.

Thank God!

You are saying this too early. She is still under pressure of marriage. Her parents are looking for another guy and Kamal wants to talk to her parents but cannot do so as even after Arjun's sister marriage you are not sure on when you will get married.

I will talk to Arjun about this.

We reached home and I was feeling too heavy in my heart. While I was thinking that I am going through the toughest relationship, my own brother was going through even worse and I felt like the reason of his troubles. I felt that for my love life I have almost killed my brother's love life. I was taking an evening walk on my terrace when my brother Kamal came to me.

If you are free, I need to talk to you sis.

Haan bol na, kya hua?

I have a girlfriend.

Yeah, I know your story. Why did you say no to her last time even without talking to anyone at home? Luckily you two have got second chance but just in case her engagement had not broken, she would have got married by now.

I know but when she asked me to talk to her parents, you were waiting for Arjun's sister to get married. Even now I am talking to you because Nitin told me his sister has got married few months back. I just want you to confirm with Arjun when you guys are planning to get married so that I can ask Naina's parents for that much time at least.

I am waiting for Arjun's call only. I will talk to him clearly today. Why don't you talk to mummy meanwhile, at least they should meet Naina's parents once.

I will do that soon.

I shared this with Arjun and warned him that if this time my brother will lose his love, Arjun will lose the same. He tried a lot to convince me but I was firm on my decision. I did not feel like talking to him more that day so disconnected the call and a baby cry came automatically out of my soul. I cursed Bhaggu a lot for bringing Arjun in life who has unintentionally turned my life upside down. He called again.

Not talking to each other cannot bring a solution, at least talk to me. We will find a solution to this too.

Solution is right here. We are getting married as soon as you complete your sailing. That's final.

It's not that easy baby. You don't know I am going through what. I have to manage you, my family and this hectic job.

Don't exaggerate baby, I do the same here. I handle everything in equal proportion, even the relatives additionally. I am not forcing you to marry, all I am saying is I will be getting married before my next birthday. You have the option of bringing the wedding procession or being a part of bride's guest list. And mind you, if we are not getting married before this then we won't get married at all.

This is not fair.

Unfair was what I have done to my brother once which I won't repeat in any case.

Achchha baba, I will talk to mom today. Scared of their reaction but one thing is for sure, it is going to bring an earthquake at my home.

I am going through this earthquake since last 3 years, now it's your turn.

Did you guys speak to the family of that girl. Meet them first, may be they will get ready to wait until you get married.

I will speak to mom about it today. Naina's father doesn't appreciate love marriages so to him it will be more of an arranged marriage.

Ok, let me know what happens.

You too. Call me after you speak to your family.

We disconnected the call and I came downstairs. Mom was busy in kitchen arranging some containers. I started my chapaati session and spoke.

Mom, did Kamal speak to you about any girl? I asked hesitatingly.

No. Which girl?

He is in love with a girl. She is from Uttarakhand only and a Brahmin too, I said.

I then told her the whole tragic story of Kamal-Naina and she got worried.

How can I even think of Kamal's marriage before your marriage, mom raised the same question.

You don't worry about me, I am getting married soon. Just talk to her mom once and see what is the situation there.

Mom, they are from Uttarakhand and are Brahmin too. Kamal and Naina know and understand each other well. What else you want?

Is not he too young?

He is young but not too young to get married.

Next day Nitin also called my mom and tried to convince her. He told her that he personally knew the girl and she is a good choice. Mom then called Naina's mother and spoke to her. Naina also had explained everything to her mother. Her mother was very soft spoken and a highly sober lady. They decided to meet on coming Friday. Her mom requested my mom to not let her husband know that it is going to be a love marriage as he was quite against love marriages. They were pretending as if the proposal has come through her parents' home. My mom then shared everything with my dad and as always he had no problem with our decision. He was happy that the girl was from same community.

Friday came and my mom-dad reached Connaught Place by 1 pm. I and Nitin joined them taking half day leave from our respective offices. We left taking auto from there and met Kamal's good friend Arjun (he too was from Bihar like my Arjun) near Naina's grandparents' residence. We went into his car and after buying some sweets and fruits, headed towards the destination.

Naina's grandparents were running a temple near to Naina's residence. It was a large farm area surrounded with many fruitful trees and flowery plants. It had a small temple in the centre and a small accommodation for them to live in. I just loved the place. We took our footwear just outside the entrance and visited temple first. We then took our seats and

117

started the conversation. After some formal talks, Naina came in the hall bringing tea; she looked decent and nice in a suit salwar with long earrings and very light make up. She had mature looks and a short height. She touched feet of my parents and we exchanged smiles. I and Nitin kept answering our official cellphones meanwhile the discussion between families went on and hence missed most of the conversation. All I could understand with whatever I heard was that they too were in favour of this marriage but they did not want to wait. Moreover they wanted to know the exact time when I will be getting married so that they can decide on when to fix their daughter's marriage. My mom however explained her everything about Arjun's problem and that his elder sister has recently got married and right now he is on ship. It might take another 4-5 months for me to get married which of course worried Naina's parents. With continuously deteriorating health of Naina's grandfather her parents did not want to wait for such a long time. On our way back to home my mom said:

They seem to be nice people, very simple and down to earth though Naina is very short heightened.

Kamal wants to marry her and if he does not have a problem with it, it should not matter at all, mom.

Did you speak to Arjun? What does he say?

He will talk to his parents today. His family expects him to marry after his brother only.

My mom reacted in the same way as I did when Arjun told me this thing as we had always been told by him that he is delaying our marriage just because his sister is due for marriage and will marry me as soon she gets married. Now

118

when my whole family is celebrating his sister's marriage as it opens up my way of getting married, this brother's-marriage-before-me drama started. My mom shared this with my sisters and as expected they all started doubting Arjun if he is really serious about our relationship or not. In all the three years of my long distance-relationship with Arjun, my most friends were not very sure about Arjun's decency and honesty. They kept warning me about this relationship which I always ignored but now the water was rising above the level. I knew Arjun was not making any excuses and he was much more serious than me in this relationship. He was not wrong in wanting his elder siblings to get married before him but now it was time for him to take the stand as I had been compromising in this relationship since last 3.5 years. I could not afford to wait for another 2-3 years. I decided to make all the things clear with Arjun that night. He called at night:

How was it? What did they say? He asked.

Did you speak to your parents?

Question in answer of a question? He said, laughing.

Just answer what I ask, I said raising my voice.

He sensed that I was in no mood of taking any jokes so he too spoke seriously.

Yeah, just before calling you I called them. I spoke to dad directly and had a verbal fight with them.

I feared this reaction from them. Anyways best of luck for your future baby. I think we were not to be with each other forever.

Don't say that. At least give me some time to convince them. It is not easy for me too.

Oh really? You need time to convince your parents about our relationship. May I ask you Mr. Tripathi what the hell you were doing since last three and half years? Just roaming around in different cities of India with a girlfriend and having fun of life.

I did not say that. You know I will marry you in any case, no matter what may come. I am just trying to convince them so that we get blessings from the entire family

I know. I am sorry for being rude these days. I don't know what is happening to me baby. I just feel like crying all the time... I said sobbing.

Please don't cry baby. I can clearly understand what you are going through. You have waited very patiently till my sister got married and were standing just beside me in these three and half years despite of facing many odds at your end. Give me some time, I will manage everything.

I trust you.

Please never stop doing that. With your love and trust, I can sail through anything. Now tell me what happened at Naina's home.

I shared everything with him and we then decided on how to go further. Arjun tried to talk about us with his parents many times after that but they always changed the topic. Meanwhile due to some unfortunate instances on ship, Arjun had a fight with his senior on ship and was asked to sign off immediately. His remaining 1.5 months contract got annulled. He was tensed as it was his first contract after the promotion, although it was not his fault which his company realized later.

12.

He came back to Mumbai but immediately started looking for another ship to join. Meanwhile he kept on trying to push his brother's marriage and also teased my topic at home whenever he got a chance. I had met everyone in Arjun's family. First I met his mom and second sister when I was in Mumbai to meet Arjun in our initial days. We met in a restaurant near his residence and they quite liked me. Once his elder sister with her husband and two kids were travelling to Mumbai via Delhi; there I met them at the railway station for few minutes. Then his parents once came to Delhi to attend some marriage function in Ghaziabad, I assisted them in taking the right bus from Delhi border. Then I met his brother who had come to Delhi to visit this guy with whom his second sister got married. I was enjoying a Delhi Dare Devil match of IPL with Mansi, Kapil and Rakesh when his brother joined us in mid of the match. All of them had accepted me well as Arjun's choice.

Arjun's sister who had recently got married was settled in Delhi now and I was in constant touch with her. I shared my brother's story with her and her husband too. Her husband was a very mature man. Arjun had asked his brother-in-law to accompany him to my house as he did not have courage to face my family alone this time. Arjun with his sister and brother-in-law came to my home and spoke to my family. The meeting went well and friendly but my sisters and mother was much serious on the marriage topic this time. My mom on a serious note also cleared that she won't wait very long for Arjun to marry me. She had even said given the ultimatum that if Arjun and Pri had not got married by July, they will have to say yes to some other proposal. My mom even cried explaining how she hears the comment of some relatives as they say "Are you delaying Priyanka's marriage because you are enjoying her earnings?" Arjun tried his best to handle the situation diplomatically and to calm my family. At last they promised to talk to Arjun's parents and fix this marriage at the earliest. My mom asked her last two questions when they were about to leave:

You have exactly 6 months to get your brother married so that you can marry my daughter. Just in case he does not get married till June end, what would you do?

I will marry Priyanka in any and every case. I just hope my brother gets married before that so that no one gets hurt with my marriage.

What if your family does not accept my daughter as their daughter in law before your brother's marriage?

Don't worry. I earn enough to settle down with your daughter anywhere on the earth.

They left and with the confidence of Arjun, my family felt a little better. Meanwhile we started receiving pressure from Naina's family as they wanted to know the maximum time we need for her and Kamal's marriage. They even came to our home to discuss further things and it was then when my mother told them that they have fixed my marriage for July so any day after my marriage they will accept Naina as their daughter-in-law.

Arjun's family still did not take things seriously and did not give importance to what Arjun was trying to say to them. They were just worried about the lifestyle and marriage of his brother. Arjun joined ship again for another four months and was scheduled to come back in the month of May. Meanwhile Arjun's brother got back in touch with his ex-girlfriend and planned to marry her in the month of June.

All my hopes started rising high again. Even his brother once called me in evening to share that he knows about mine and Arjun's problem and also told me that he is now all set for marriage and after he gets married in June, we can get married in July. I was so happy that I instantly shared this with my mom who was then speaking on phone with our family pundit. She asked him to suggest an auspicious date for my marriage in the month of July. We all were too happy and I waited for Arjun's call to share this with him. He called at night:

I was waiting for your call only, I spoke.

No more bad news please.

Jo hukum maalik, I have good news for a change.

I am shocked. It seems good things have stopped coming to us.
Oh shut up, don't talk like a loser. The news is your brother called me in the evening today. He said he is getting married by June so we can plan our marriage for next month.

Getting married with his girlfriend?

Yes.

Forget it then. They are doing this since last 8 years. They patch up for a month and then break up for two. They won't get married, you take that in writing.

I got numb as all my happiness swept away in fraction of seconds. He sensed my reaction and spoke again:

Don't worry; I will talk to my elder brother-in-law tonight. He is quite mature and I am sure he will help me in convincing my parents for us. You take care of urself. I saw your latest photos on Facebook and you are looking much slimmer. I am gaining weight day by day and you are losing it in equal proportion. Shaadi to teri mujhse hi hogi baby.

Only if you will be able to convince your family soon, I replied.
You go and sleep now. I will call you tomorrow to share what they said.

I disconnected and came downstairs. Felt like sharing Arjun's feedback on his brother's idea of marriage with mom but could not do so seeing her smiling face. She was so happy with the thought that everything has fallen in place so I waited for the right time to talk to her.

Meanwhile when I was embattled in my own love story, Mansi's parents were tired of finding a good match for her. Her friendly Mausi maa asked her many times if she likes anyone but her answer was "No" always. Finally one day Mansi shared about her friend Raj with her Mausi. Raj was her old friend who used to like Mansi since last 9 years but she always treated him as her good friend only. Raj was an average looking guy from some small town of Uttar Pradesh (Pilibhit) but was in Delhi for his job and studies. He was the only son of his parents who were living in Pilibhit. He was preparing for some government jobs since last many years. He was bright in studies but due to his hard luck he could not crack his exams with the shortage of 2-3 marks mostly.

He had recently cleared his exams for government job and was given an opportunity with LIC (Life Insurance

Company) which he grabbed with no further delay. Mansi shared about him after seeing he is now settled with a good job. Mansi's Mausi took great interest in her loving niece and convinced her parents to talk to Raj and his family. In no time, everything was fixed and she was getting married in the month of March. I was happy for her but also felt bad for she will be going far away from me. We had a gala time with her pre-wedding fun. Went to all places we wanted to, thinking it may be the last time we are getting this chance. We spent hours in shopping her marriage stuffs.

One day we were discussing after-marriage life with our one of the married colleague in office when I received my mom's call. She told me that pundit has suggested 7th July as the best date for my marriage and 9th July for Kamal as after these two dates there was no auspicious time till the month of October. She asked me to share it with Arjun and let her know if he is ok with it or not. I disconnected the phone saying I will get married on 7th July only. I sent a text to Arjun asking him to call me as soon as possible. He called me after 30 minutes:

What happened? Is everything alright?

That depends on how you take what I have to say.

Sounds like something is really serious.

As per our Pundit, we can either get married on 7th July or directly after October. Before you say we can wait until October, you should know Naina's parents are not waiting for Kamal. They have clearly told us that they want her daughter to get married at the earliest. They are very much happy with sending her daughter to our home but they won't stop looking for other options until we give them a specific

126

date for their marriage.

Why are they in such a hurry?

Why are you so lenient on this? Sometimes I really doubt if you love me or not. You know I have waited for three and half years for your sister to get married, avoiding so many questions and even taunts from everybody about my marriage. Now, when it is the question of my brother's love which he has already lost once just because of you and me, you don't even take it seriously.

You do not understand my problem. Your brother is still younger to you and I am worrying about my elder brother's marriage.

Yeah, elder brother who himself is not sure by when he will get married or if he will ever do that or not.

You are right but even I am not wrong. You can't imagine what havoc it will bring if we get married before my brother.

I understand everything baby; especially after 3.5 years of this relationship I think I understand you very much. That is why I am not forcing you for anything, just telling you if you are not comfortable in getting married in July, you are free to go. I will get married on 7th July and that's final.

You know Pri, I can't live without you.

You should know I will not let my brother lose his love once again because of me. Not in any case.

I disconnected the phone in anger and resumed back to my workplace. I shared everything with Rohan and Mansi and cried.

I didn't like to hurt Arjun at all but I too was going through such a trauma that I was left with no other option. My mom asked me about Arjun's input on this Pundit's suggestion to which I replied "I didn't get time to talk to him during office hours, so I will talk to him at night"

I was afraid. I was afraid of losing Arjun. I was afraid of ruining my brother's love life once again. I was afraid of getting miffed relations after marriage. My head kept spinning until I answered Arjun's call.
Tell your mom I will marry you on 7th July.

I sensed the tension and anger in his words so asked "All ok?"

Just had a fight with my dad and elder sister. My dad is not at all ready to hear anything. He has clearly told me that if I want to get married, I can but he will not be present there. Everyone is ready to give advices but no one wants to understand what we are going through. You just tell your mother to fix everything, I will come to Delhi directly if my family does not want to be a part of our marriage and we will stay in Delhi only after marriage. I will come in the month of June and rent an apartment for us.

I didn't want this to happen baby, I am really sorry. I don't know what to do or say. I know none of us is wrong but all of us are suffering.

Why are you crying? It's not your fault. You have done a lot in these three and half years. I am angry for my family's reaction. I am shocked to see that they are fine if I lose my love.

Calm down. Just talk to your brother-in-law; both of them are very understanding. I am sure they will understand you and will suggest a solution.

Ok. I will try but we will get married on 7th July and that's final now.

I shared this with my mother. She tried to convince Naina's parents to wait for some more time but they politely denied. Naina's mother said "Her father's concern is to get Naina married ASAP and not to get her married with Kamal" She also told my mother that Naina's father is going to see a guy for her next weekend and if everything goes well, he might fix it there only. My mom got worried and so did Kamal and I. Meanwhile Arjun spoke to his both brother-in-laws. They promised him to talk to his father and try to convince him. His elder brother-in-law (Aakash jiju) was in full favour of our decision as he was tired of seeing Arjun's elder brother changing his mind on marriage since last many years. His younger brother-in-law (Aashish jiju) was trying to fix things at both the ends. On his brother-in-law's suggestion, Arjun asked me to convince my parents to talk to his parents so that the matter goes serious. I followed the same and my mother called Arjun's mother.

My mom had already talked to Arjun's mother earlier but she kept avoiding the marriage topic. This time my mom clearly spoke about marriage stuff. She shared everything about Kamal also and requested her to take this matter seriously now. Arjun's mother did not talk much and handed over the phone to Arjun's father. My mom spoke to him for few minutes and found him very rude so she handed over the phone to my father. My father tried to explain things to Arjun's father but he was too arrogant to listen anything. He

129

did not give any chance to my parents to utter a word. My father was a very soft spoken person and he did not like the way Arjun's dad was talking so he disconnected the phone and asked my mother to talk and tell them if they are not happy with this relation, we will get our daughter married somewhere else. My mom called back again and spoke to Arjun's father in detail this time. He told her that they all like Arjun's choice and ready to accept me as their daughter-in-law but not before their elder son's marriage. He even invited my parents to Mumbai to have a brief discussion on this. My mom then disconnected the phone.

I went to ask her what did they say and found her crying. She hugged me said "I am so worried for you beta. I don't think they will ever be ready for this marriage". I replied "Why are you worried then, I will get what is there in my fate and I am sure it will be best for me". My dad joined and said crying "I would have fixed your marriage in a much better family if I was working or I had some savings for you. This dowry system has tied my hands and I feel so helpless". I could not hold my tears seeing my mom dad crying for me. I ran to terrace and cried out loud there. I controlled my emotions as Arjun was calling me and ended in crying even louder as his first question was "did your father spoke to mine?" I shared everything with him and requested him to leave me and find someone else for him so that he does not have to hurt his family and I don't hurt mine. He did not find it a good solution and said:
Listen Pri, I did not fall in love with you with my parents' permission. I can't leave you now and can't even live without you. We will get married in July only. It is our duty to ask them and we did it. I can't sacrifice my love for their conservative mentality of marrying only elder son first.

Swear yar baby, I don't understand what's wrong in marrying

130

younger son first. Who cares now about who got married when? I mean for a girl I would have understood the concern and we did that. We did wait for your sister to marry first. Remember my maternal uncle from Punjab. His younger son got married before the elder one and today both are married happily with one child of both. On top of that now your brother also is planning to marry in June. What's wrong now?

He is not marrying his girlfriend now. They broke up.

Oh my god! Are these people crazy or what?

Remember I told you their relationship status changes even before the month. Don't worry, I will talk to Aakash and Aashish jiju now and tell them clearly that I am getting married in the month of July and will stay in Delhi if they don't want to accept our marriage.

Arjun discussed everything with his brother-in-law. He promised him to try again to convince Arjun's father. He went to Arjun's home and explained everything to his parents. They patiently listened this time and even told him that they are not against our marriage but they are worried about how Arjun's brother will react after consuming alcohol. He had already created scenes many times since this topic was being discussed. During the day his brother was sober, matured and understanding but at night after having a drink he was totally the opposite. His family was just trying to avoid this and said they would like to meet my parents to discuss everything face to face. Arjun conveyed same to me. My mom, dad, Priya di and Nitin agreed to go. I arranged their tickets costing INR 25000. I calculated my remaining savings. I had been saving money from my second job for my marriage. It was hard to save much as I was the only earning member in my home since I started working. After giving the major amount of my salary to mom for household expenses and keeping something for my own personal expenses, I saved whatever was possible. Arjun and I had always planned for a simple marriage keeping my savings in mind. Now I had to arrange Kamal's marriage also out of this savings of mine.

13.

Finally the day came when they had to leave for Mumbai. I gave the contact number of Arjun's father, brother and Aakash jiju to Nitin. Also gave Nitin's and my dad's contact number to Aakash jiju who had promised to pick my parents from the railway station. I went to see off my family at the station and found my mother with a worrying face. I could sense the fear of getting insulted again. I told Nitin and Priya di in front of my mom dad to hear and bear to an extent only. I even asked them to reply back rudely if they initiate so. I left station hoping for the best to happen.

Arjun spoke to his elder Aakash jiju number of times to say "please take care of everything there". My parents reached on time and met Arjun's brother-in-law at the station. Aakash jiju kept on describing every member of Arjun's family to them so that they get a better idea of how to talk to whom. I called to ensure if they have reached safely and requested my mummy to talk softly but not to accept any non-sense rudeness of anyone for my sake. I prayed for a healthy conversation of them all. They were all looking not-so-fresh after a whole night train travel so first thing they did was to get freshen-up in Arjun's home. I sent a message to Nitin on whatsApp to keep updating me. He instantly replied with a call back. I answered asking:

All ok?

Yeah, just had bath and now waiting for them to start the conversation. He handed over phone to mummy saying "talk to tai-ji"

Haan mummy, kya chal raha hai?

133

Nothing. They have a guest here who had fixed their younger daughter's marriage and these people do not seem interested in talking in front of him, mom whispered tenderly.

Where are you? Are not those hearing you saying all this?

No, we are in inner most room taking rest. Arjun's mom has gone to some nearby temple and father is busy with that guest.

That's rude. Tell them we don't have a week to talk and need to travel back tonight.

Let Arjun's mom come back, we will talk then.

Ok, give phone to Priya di.

Yeah sis, Di spoke in her usual funny tone.

Arjun told me his father is bit rude and talks a lot and our mum seems to be of same species. Just take care if these two don't start any world war.

Don't worry sis, everything will be alright.

I hung up the phone but with a bit of anger for how Arjun's parents were behaving.

I wished I was there to protect my family's pride in case Arjun's family gets rude as no matter how much I loved Arjun, my family was always my priority. I still remember the day my father almost killed my elder sister for asking to marry a Bengali boy and how my mother asked her to choose between parents or that boy. How my elder sisters were not allowed to wear short or fancy western dresses. I was

134

fortunate to have their mentality changed in my case. I wore whatever I liked and now they are even ready to get me married in a distant city to a boy of Bihar. They didn't let me down when I asked to marry a guy of my choice. How can I do this to them? If anyone of my family gets hurt because of Arjun's family I won't spare anyone, I swore in my head.

I tried to stay busy in whatever I could do but only with my physical presence as my mind was continuously running towards the families meet.
After 4 hours of long wait and with the loss of almost all my nails I got a call from Nitin again. I answered with all the expressions of the world.

Haan Nitin, kya hua?

It's me, mom spoke from there.

Yeah mom, what's happening? I asked trying not to sound nervous.
Just finished talking. Oh sorry, not talking. It was more of "Just listening".

I sensed the anger in her voice, so asked politely if everything was ok.

I don't understand why they invited us here to talk when Arjun's dad never allows anyone to talk. Forget about us, he didn't even allow his own family members to say a word. I am still asking you to think about your decision once again. You deserve much better beta.

Mom, stop behaving dramatically. Tell me properly what happened.

Mummy: It's not good to explain things from here. We will call you after taking the train.

Ok. What are you doing now?

Just had lunch so taking rest in that same room. I think they too are discussing things in other room.

Let them do what they want to, I said furiously.

Ok, bye for now.

I hung up and went to Mansi's home to divert my mind. Time had never been so slow in past 27 years. I checked my watch after every 30 minutes and it showed only 5 minutes has been passed. I and Mansi discussed every possibility that could have happened in that family meet. My ultimate energy booster was Maggi so I bought a pack of maggi on my way back to home. While having maggi I felt a fear in a corner of my heart that this may be the end of my love story and I may have to choose one between Arjun and my family. My thoughts fell apart with my mobile's ringtone. It was Nitin. I wiped my tears and answered the phone keeping my fingers crossed.

Hello.

Hello darling. We have just boarded the train. Aakash jiju came to drop us back.

Ok. Is he still there?

No, he just left.

So, what happened there?

Better you talk with tai-ji.

Mummy took phone and asked "what time this train will reach Delhi?"

Don't change the topic. What happened there?

We tried our best to convince them but they are not ready to let

Arjun marry first and on top of that they do not know till when he is going to marry. So the point is you should wait for Arjun even if it takes 3-4 years for his brother to get married but you don't worry beta, you wait. You wait for Arjun because you want to marry him only. We will keep answering and handling various taunts of relatives and neighbours about not marrying you, mom said and started crying.

Priya di took the phone as soon as she heard mom crying. I could hear Nitin consoling mom in the background. I could not react. Priya di spoke on phone.

Hello sis.

Yeah di. At least you tell me what exactly happened there.

Arey nothing serious. Let us come back, we will tell you everything.
What's wrong in telling me now? Please tell me.

They are not at all ready to let Arjun marry first. You were saying Arjun's brother called you and asked you to get married as he will be marrying soon too?

Yeah, he did.

He clearly said in presence of all that he may not marry his girlfriend and not sure when exactly he will get married and to whom. Everything is uncertain with them except one thing that their younger son is in love with you, unfortunately. Arjun's father said we are trying to manipulate his son and that we are forcing him to marry you otherwise he does not want to get married. Moreover he was very rude yar. He was literally shouting during most of the conversation.

What you all did then? Didn't you answer the same way? I asked angrily.

Come on sis, we didn't want to fight with them.

What were they doing then?

They just said what they want and we conveyed what we want, that's it. My advice to you is take a decision as fast as you can. Talk to Arjun, if his parents are not ready, it is better for you two to move on.

I didn't know how to react on what Priya di just said so just made an excuse of another call and disconnected the line. After few minutes got an SMS from Nitin which read "Oye, don't worry.

Everything will be all right. We will talk after coming back. Don't take any decision in anger".

Arjun didn't call that night as he was sailing and was out of network. Mom came back next day. Priya di was washing the

138

utensils, they brought back from their travel and then we spoke. Arjun's mom is very sweet. She insisted a lot to take food with us for train. Taste this pickle, isn't it yummy.

What did she have to say on your discussion? I asked expecting a positive answer.

She was very polite but uncle rarely gave her any chance to speak. Everytime anyone said anything against his words, he started to shout. Leave us, he even kept on shouting on his wife and Aakash ji. Arjun's elder sister and her husband are nice people too. Vaibhav too seemed very mature when spoke. This alcohol, I am telling you, it ruins everything. What is his age? I don't understand why is he doing all this?

Because he is not interested in getting married to a decent girl and leave that girl who fights with him every alternate day. He is not only addicted to alcohol, he seems to be in addiction of that girl. Whatever, I don't give a damn now.

Did you speak to Arjun about it? Nitin entered in kitchen and asked.

No, not yet. I have decided I will not marry Arjun now. I will tell him clearly that I don't want to get into that house without the consent of his family members which does not seem possible to me anymore.

It hurts but I think it will be good in long run for both of you. You can't stay happy in such a house where people don't accept you heartedly, Nitin said lowering his voice.

Right bro and as they all say "Nobody dies without anyone". So won't we.

Just when I completed my sentence, mom entered too asking "who is dying without whom?" Nitin told her about my decision and she left saying "der aaye durust aaye" (She meant better late than never, finally I got brains to take this decision). During lunch mom started the topic again.

I can't forget the way Arjun's father was talking. So rude of a person he is. Tu shaadi kar bhi legi na to khush nahi rahegi wahaan, I am telling you.

Leave it now; she said she will talk to Arjun, Priya Di tried to stop mom.

Why should I leave it? You don't know what his father said to your dad. When your dad told them that our pundit has suggested the dates of 7th and 9th July for both the marriages, he spoke to your dad in a tone which I can't even explain. He said "how dare you to take out the marriage date without our consent. We are ladke wale, how could you do anything without our permission"

I think he didn't mean to be that rude and he talks like that always, Nitin tried to calm mom down.

How did you end the topic, I mean what was the outcome of the discussion? I asked Priya di.

Honestly sis, outcome was nothing. On one hand they kept on insisting to marry Arjun after his brother and on other hand they agreed to marry you and Arjun in November.

And what if his brother does not get married by November also? I asked.

Still they will let you and Arjun marry, I mean this is what they are saying. Nitin replied.

So what is the problem now? Are not their relatives going to question after November "why Arjun got married first and not Vaibhav?" If in July they have this concern then how come they are ready for November even if Vaibhav doesn't get married? I asked to which mom replied:

This is what I asked because they have not even seen a girl for Vaibhav till yet. He is also planning to go for sailing in few days. Then how come it is possible for him to get married by November.
What did they say then? I asked.

They didn't have any answer so just kept on saying in November we will handle anyhow, mom said passing the water bottle to Nitin.
They are not going to handle this in November also. They all are afraid of Vaibhav as he creates ruckus after drinking. He will do that in November also if we marry before him. They are just giving excuses to shirk this July matter, I said in anger.

Dekh beta, I am even ready for November also but the decision is on you.

You know it well mom, I am not insisting to get married in July because I am dying to marry Arjun. We have been in this relationship for four years and I can even take it few months further before we get married. I am doing so because Naina's parents have given time limit upto July only. Kamal and Naina have already gone through a lot because of me and Arjun, I don't want them to suffer anymore because of me. I am getting married in July and that's final. If not with Arjun then with someone else but this 7th July is fixed for my

141

marriage and 9th for Kamal. You call Naina's parents and tell them to start their preparations and you also start yours.

Priya Di and Nitin left in afternoon after lunch as they had to join offices next day. Mom got busy in household chores and I pretended to sleep but in mind kept thinking about the things I will have to tell Arjun to bring this to an end. I swear on Arjun, it was hurting too badly to even think about it but that was the way I think it was meant to be. Arjun called at night, I had not spoken to him since last 2 days.

Where the hell are you? He asked angrily as soon as I answered the call.

Why? You were not in reach and you are shouting on me.

Madam, check your phone. I have been calling you since I got network. You didn't answer my 3 calls.

Really? I said looking at my phone. He was right. My phone was displaying 5 missed calls out of which 3 was of him.

Yes really. When you didn't answer I called at home and spoke to dad and mom as I was curious to know the outcome of their meeting.

What did they say? I asked to know their perspective.

That everything has been sorted out and your parents are ready for November.

What the fuck? Who said that?

What? You mean to say it is not true. He asked in confusion.

No, it is not true at all. They never said they are ready for

November, they just left your home saying we will discuss with our relatives and let you know. They had to say it because your father was too rude to accept any other thing. Whenever my family members said anything related to marriage in July, your father started shouting. He has even said if we marry in July, he will not attend it and even if he attends it, he will sit facing walls but not us in any case. I said, literally shouting to the maximum.

I can't believe it but first you calm down baby and tell me in detail what happened there.

I am sorry baby, I didn't want to shout on you. I know you are equally tensed these days, may be much more than me. I said lowering my voice and explained him everything what happened there.

"Hmm" was his only response. He didn't have much to say after listening me, so I only continued.

Listen baby, I think it is high time for us to part our ways. You know everything, most importantly you know me. You know baby, since my parents lost their first son, they just hoped for a baby boy and nothing else. After giving birth to four daughters they finally got Kamal. We all have loved him so much since then. Four of us never celebrated our birthday just because we wanted our parents to have enough money to celebrate Kamal's birthday revelry. We have always sacrificed the best piece of cake for our only brother. I have given up on many of my hobbies and belongings for him. And today my brother had to break up with the only girl he ever fell in love just because of me. He has luckily got second chance to marry her now after her engagement didn't last with the guy which her parents fixed for her. I don't want to snatch this opportunity from them again. I can't be the reason of his same sorrow again. My brother sacrificed his love life once for me and now it's time for me to return the favour to him. I have decided, I am getting married on 7th July and they will marry on 9th. I don't want to force you for anything as I understand your family's concern though I don't agree with them. Let's stop it here and break it up.

I got it. Now it's my turn to speak and you better don't interrupt until I ask you to. Arjun said in his usual matured and firm voice.

First of all, I don't agree with this solution of yours. Secondly, your parents' job is done after they have tried enough of times to talk to my parents. Thirdly, I didn't love you with anyone's permission so I don't need anyone's permission to marry also. Fourthly, I appreciate your feelings for your brother and this decision of yours. I know you have already waited for 4 years in order to let my sister marry first so it's time for me to help you in getting your brother married to his love. And the last, I love you too much baby. I can't even think of living without you now. You are the reason I want to leave all my bad habits. You are the reason I have started loving myself. You are the reason I care now for how I look. You are the reason I can die for and I mean it.

Please baby, I can fight with everyone if only you are with me. Be with me and I promise you will never regret it.

He stopped speaking hearing my cry on the other side. I just could not resist crying a loud, nor could I speak.

Say something, please. He spoke again.

I love you too baby. I just don't want you to go against your parents to marry me. I said trying to control my wail.

Listen baby, both of us wanted this marriage to happen with our family's consent and that's why we never spoke to them about our marriage in last four years. Now when we really need to, we have already tried enough of times to convince them. They know the reason we want to get married. It's not that I am marrying you without thinking of anyone. We did wait for 4 long years so that my sister gets married first and it was necessary as we live in a society where people are very much concerned for why younger sibling had to marry if elder sister is still at home. You never asked me to get married until my sister was unmarried even when your family and relatives kept pressurizing you for marriage. You handled all that alone but never left my side and today when it's time for me to be with you, you are asking me to leave. You forgot that song I dedicated once to you "Hum bane tum bane ik dooje ke liye, usko kasam lage jo bichhad ke ik pal bhi jiye"

I remember. You remember the song I dedicated in return of it? I asked… finally smiling.

I remember everything honey. It was "Ek tamanna jeevan ki main pyar tera hi paun, shaadi tujh hi se ho meri chahe shaadi ke din mar jaun" By the way if you die on the day of marriage, what will happen to our first night? What is the benefit of getting married then? Huh! He teased.

You Dog, you will never change.

Thank god, you stopped crying. Everything has a solution, just be strong and bear with me. I will handle everything. He said.

What do we do now? Mom is worried too.

145

I will talk to aunty, you don't worry. Just ask her to call my mom one last time and tell her that we cannot wait until November so let us know if you are not ready for this marriage, I will find another match for my daughter. And let me know what they say in reply. I will call at home after that.

Ok. I will call you later then.

I am waiting. He said and hung up.

I came down from terrace and told mom everything what Arjun had to say. She said she doesn't mind this marriage if Arjun is ready and his family isn't but this will be his responsibility to manage my relationship with other family members if we are going to stay with them. She then called Arjun's mom and spoke to her.

My mom: Namaste behanji.

His mom: Namaste, kaun?

My mom: I am Priyanka's mom speaking. Behenji I am not feeling good to say this but we can't wait till November and as discussed at your home you guys are not ready for marriage in July so with consent of all we have decided to start finding another match for Priyanka.

His mom: Behenji don't take such hard decision hastening.

My mom: I am helpless behanji. I have to get my son married this July and he won't marry before Priyanka. I have discussed everything in detail with our close relatives and they all have suggested this only. Even Priyanka has agreed with our decision. I just wanted to inform you so called up at this time. Rakhti hun behanji, namaste.

She disconnected phone and said looking at me "they all understand that this elder-brother-should-marry-first is not that big of an issue in today's era especially if it is a love marriage. They are making this issue just because they are afraid of Arjun's brother's reaction. Elders are afraid of younger in that home, kaise rahegi tu wahaan pata nahi".

I called Arjun and told him about our mothers' conversation. We then discussed a few things that we may have to handle if we marry against his family's wish. It was getting late and I had office next day so I disconnected the call soon after that and slept thanking Bhaggu for bringing a guy in my life who loves me beyond my expectations.

Arjun then spoke to almost all his family members including sisters and their husbands. Aakash jiju and Aashish jiju were in our favour. Aakash jiju talked to Arjun's brother and asked clearly if he is really willing to marry his girlfriend as they could get him marry before July so that Arjun's marriage will not be a problem for him anymore. He denied saying I will take time to marry. Aakash jiju also tried to convince Arjun's parents for our marriage but all in vain as they were stuck to Vaibhav's marriage first. When Aakash jiju got to know that my parents have decided to see some other guy for me and still Arjun's parents are not in favour of this marriage, he got really angry for how selfish they were behaving. Arjun then in anger announced his decision that no matter what he is going to marry in July with me. All are invited and if nobody is willing to come and accept us both after marriage, he will go for court marriage and will stay at some other place after marriage.

Arjun called me at night and shared everything that happened at his home. I too got upset for how smooth it was

147

going until few days before. My family was so happy with my choice and Arjun's family with his choice. Arjun was sounding too low and that made me say that again.

Arjun don't you think we should think about it once again.

What do you mean?

I mean will we really be able to live a content life if we marry against their will?

I don't know about living a content life but I am sure about living my life with you and don't you dare talk to me again about break-up possibilities.

Ok fine but what should I tell my mom. She needs to do the preparations for marriage function. How are we going to marry, in a court or the banquet hall?

Even I am not sure baby. If my family changes their mind we will marry in banquet otherwise we will go for court marriage, he said very much confused.

We have very few days remaining and we may not get banquet hall if we book it so late. You know three banquet halls which are near us are all booked for whole July month, same with caterers, decorators and DJ etc.

I know yar Pri but you know my situation.

I will ask mom to start her preparations, we will cancel those if it does not happen that way.

That would be fine. You know I am not on talking terms with anyone in my family. Let's see if threat of court marriage and living separately and my sadness affects them somehow.

Hoping so baby, fine then I will catch you later. Need to help mom in kitchen.

14.

I asked my mom to start the preparations but didn't tell her that there are chances of court marriage too as she could have started cursing Arjun's family again. However, Arjun's threat worked like magic. After few more days of discussions cum arguments cum debates finally they all were ready for the marriage including Vaibhav bhaiya. I started getting updates from Arjun for what all they are buying for me. Arjun knew my taste and that I did not generally like only-for-girls-things. He tried his best to restrain his mother and sister from buying heavy Saree and jewellery for me.

One late night I received a text message from Rakesh which read "can I call you, if you are not sleeping?" I called him back.

All ok buddy? I asked

Yeah, wanted to share one good and one bad news.

Go ahead.

I am getting married.

Wow, that certainly is good news. Congratulations. What is the bad news then?

4th July is the date.
So what?

Idiot, 4th July means you will not be able to attend my marriage and I can't attend yours. You forgot you are getting married on 7th July?
Oh no! This is truly a bad news buddy. Can't you shift your date a little?

I tried yar but this seems to be the best date as per our horoscopes and you know my family.

Yeah, anyways I am happy for you. We will fix some get together post marriage.

Definitely! I will call you tomorrow; you better go to sleep now.

Ok. Good night, sleep well.

I am in office darling, night shifts. He said mocking cry.

I shared this with Arjun and he too felt bad for he knew I and Rakesh were best friends and Arjun and I had kept Lucknow pending in our travel list as we knew we will anyway go to Lucknow someday when Rakesh will get married.

Anyways, Arjun and I were very happy for once again the things were smooth between us and finally we were getting married. We had so much to talk about now, from marriage preparations to honeymoon to family planning. We even finalized Mauritius for our honeymoon and I started finding the packages for it. I got it booked through Nitin's company. We both were on cloud nine when Arjun's parents insisted on a ritual of theirs' in which bride's family is supposed to give many gifts, clothes, money etc to the groom. My family did not take it positively as we did not have any such ritual to follow in our custom. Being honest even I did not like this idea as I had shared everything about our financial condition with Arjun before coming into this relationship. He very well knew that only with my savings we are going to perform these marriages. I spoke to him about it in the evening:

151

What is this now baby? You know everything still you are asking for this function, I asked furiously.

I tried to convince them yar but you know how they have agreed for this marriage. I could not force them.

So you decided to force my family for this, I continued in anger.

You are taking me wrong baby. There should be some solution to this problem too, he replied thinking too hard to find some solution.

After a pause he suggested that we send all the gifts and clothes on the day of that ritual instead of giving them on wedding day which was acceptable to me as we anyway had to give those things to them.

What about the cash that we are supposed to give you in that ritual? How much you guys are expecting, I asked raising my eyebrows.

Expecting? Come on baby, don't talk as if we are asking for dowry.

What else it is then? Isn't a ritual where we need to give gifts and cash to would-be-groom and his family an indirect way of asking for dowry?

Fine. It may be an indirect dowry but for now we have to follow it baby for the sake of our marriage. Please! If you don't mind I can help you with money, he said giving another solution.

Don't you dare do that. We will do the arrangements as per our capabilities even if it means we give you rupee one in that function. You want a lavish function; arrange a large

152

reception in Mumbai but how much we will spend in the function which is being arranged by us will be our decision.

Ok Lady Bheem, as you say. Now cheer up and change the topic. Tell me if you are done with your shopping for honeymoon. I have already started imagining you in those sexy dresses, he sighed.
I smiled as I knew he was just trying to change my mood.

It took me time to convince my mom as she was against giving cash in that ritual but at last she was fine with it. Everyone in my family was too busy in running for some or the other work as they had to do arrangements for two functions, one being ladke wale another being ladki wale.

Arjun came to Delhi for making arrangements of accommodation and caterers for the wedding as they were going to stay near his sister's residence in Delhi. We met and did some shopping together. We were happy once again and I prayed we don't get any other problem now which was difficult for Bhaggu to fulfil as he had some chronic issues with me. Another issue we faced was marriage date. As per Arjun's family they could not carry any auspicious function on Tuesday (they believed Tuesday to be a cursed day as Arjun's grandfather died on a Tuesday) which was 8th July when my farewell was scheduled. Having only few days left in marriage they said they are ready for the marriage on 7th July as it will be Monday but they will not take the bride along with them as by the time marriage will be solemnised it will turn to be Tuesday.

I could not resist my anger when Arjun came up to me with this. I seriously felt as if his family is just trying to cancel this marriage somehow.

153

Let's face it baby, your parents are still not ready for our marriage. All they are doing is just creating one mess after another.

It's not like that. I always knew about this Tuesday thing but never noticed that we are marrying on Monday which will be ending with a farewell on Tuesday. I know they are not lying.

Fine but I am tired of convincing my family now. What do I tell them? Mom I am getting married but unlike all other Indian brides I will not leave with groom after marriage, rather I will come back to home with you all. Can you imagine how disgraceful it will be for me to come back to my own house after my farewell? Have you ever seen a marriage like this?

I understand and that's why I have called to find some solution baby.

Solution! Solution! Solution! Why do we have to have a problem at very first instance? It feels as if even Bhaggu is against this marriage.

No, with every solution we get for our problems that raised it seems even Bhaggu wants this marriage to happen. He said trying to calm me but I was too upset to understand anything. I disconnected the phone to discuss this with my family. As expected they all reacted like me hearing this.

Are you sure Arjun's family is ready for the marriage, Nitin asked?

I know yar, I too asked the same question to Arjun but they are not lying about this Tuesday thing. Arjun told me how they have always shifted their programmes that were falling on some Tuesday.

Whatever! It is not possible for you to come back with us after your farewell. Neighbours and relatives are going to laugh on us. They are already against this Pahadi-Bihari marriage. In any case they don't have to take you to Mumbai as you will have to stay back in Delhi to attend Kamal's marriage. Can't they take you to Arjun's sister's place also? My mom said.

I will talk to Arjun about this, I said and left the conversation which continued even after that for another 1 hour. I was about to call Arjun when I received Bharti's call, she had shifted to Jaipur few months back. She just called to say that she will not be able to come and attend my marriage which turned my mood to even worse. I called Arjun and gave him the logic which my mom had given.

What do you think Pri? We have not discussed this at home? Mom said we can't take bride along with us on Tuesday be it to Mumbai or to anywhere.

You and your bloody beliefs are going beyond my tolerance Arjun. They are right who say one should not marry beyond his caste and religion. First your family's conservative thinking of getting only elder son marry first, then ladke wale are superior to ladki wale mindset, then those expensive rituals and now this good for nothing belief. I regret my decision of marrying you baby. I never thought I will have to hurt my family so much for a guy. My parents are going to marry their one and only son whom not only they but we all have loved most. Come and see if you find any happiness on their old faces because I don't. Every time I go in front of them they get afraid that I might have got some other issues to tell them.

I could not speak more and started crying a loud.

155

Please don't cry baby. I really understand what you are going through because of me but I am equally helpless and you know that. You know Vaibhav has agreed for this marriage in pressure of all but he still is very much against it. Every alternate night he is coming fully drunk and is creating scenes at home. He abuses mom, dad, sisters and even both brother-in-laws as they have agreed for our marriage. I have not slept well since last many nights and in day time we have to do the preparations of marriage. I talk to you to cheer up my mood and here we also have started fighting regularly. Let's leave all this and get married in court. I just want you to be happy no matter how.

I am sorry baby. I know you are at no fault still I keep on taking out my anger on you. I just really don't know what to do now as my family will never agree for this no matter how hard I try and same with your family. After distributing cards all over we can't let our parents down and go for court marriage. Give me some time; let me try to find some solution for this and you also think if you get some idea. We will talk at night, I said.

Ok but I am clueless for now. How about preparations of your brother's marriage? I hope they guys are not facing such problems like us.

It is going fine. Fortunately, they belong to same caste and religion.
I called Mansi to change my mood. She told me that her tickets have been booked and she will be in Delhi before my Mehendi ceremony. I felt a little better as I was afraid that if Bharti is not coming from Jaipur when she lives with her husband alone, it would be difficult for Mansi also to come as she was living in Uttar Pradesh with her in-laws. On top of

that she was newly married but she managed it somehow. I shared with her about this new problem and together we found out a brilliant solution. I discussed that with my family first, they liked it then I called Arjun to share that with him.

Found some solution or not? I asked just to tease him.

No baby, I am really tensed. I think we have to go for court marriage now, he replied in frustration.

I laughed and said "I have found one and mom is ok with it".

Oh my god! Are you serious?

Yes, I am serious. See what I have decided is after my farewell you just get me into your car and drop me to my Mausi's home which is just 5 minutes drive from the banquet hall and also on your way back to your sister's home. I will take some rest there till evening as we have to be in my home for Kamal's Mehendi and DJ party. You can directly come to Mausi's place in evening so that we can leave for my home together. This way, neither you are taking me home nor are my parents taking me back with them.

What an idea Priyanka ji. I love you tooooooooooo much baby, he said in excitement.

I love you too. Now share this with your family if they are ok with it or not.

They will have to, otherwise....

Otherwise we will go for court marriage; I interrupted and completed his sentence. We both laughed.

15.

After a fun filled musical Mehendi night, finally the big day arrived. The day started with "Ganesh Pooja" followed by "Haldi Rasm". By the afternoon most people were running from one place to another for some or the other work. Nitin and Kamal were constantly on phone arranging things in the banquet hall. I had to leave for parlour to get my bridal makeup done. The girls at the parlour were so amused to see my bridal lehenga which was a combined choice of Arjun and mine. Unlike usual red, it was of golden colour with peacock design wherever it suited. I had arranged the matching jewellery and chooda also, both with peacock design. For a moment, I kind of laughed on me, thinking how this bride feeling has changed me.

I was happy but those tiring hours of parlour made me hate make-up even more. Seeing myself in mirror I was remembering the day when one of my friends asked me "which of your photo is your favourite?" and I answered "that is yet to be clicked, that would be in my bridal look" I think I was looking good but not that much how those parlour girls were reacting. I let it go thinking that's part of their job to praise girls, their masters have worked on. Ladies were working on my bridal bun which was taking a hell lot of time that made me lose patience as I was tired of moving my head and neck in all the directions enabling them to get a perfect bun. I was also wondering if I will ever get my hair in normal shape after witnessing all the knots they had made in my hair, fixing them with some spray.

I asked for water just to give my neck a little rest and that's when I received a call of Nitin. I spoke without giving him a chance to speak "Dulhan ko time lagega abhi, have some patience" He just replied saying "good, take your time. You may have to wait there for a little long". He disconnected the phone leaving me in fear of what could have happened. I was about to ask that lady to start her work when I received dad's call.

Where are you? He asked

I am in parlour dad. What happened? Is everything OK?

Nothing is fine here. I just reached the banquet hall to ensure things are all set and what I am seeing here is not at all ready banquet hall. Arjun's brother in law called to inform they have already left for our place. Workers here are saying they are not allowed to do anything without owner's permission and that idiot is not answering his phone. Dad said in one breath.

I called Nitin back and asked him about this. He started uttering non-stop abuses for that tent house owner. I got worried for dad's health as he had high BP problem. Nitin ensured me that he is on the way to banquet and he will get the things arranged soon. I asked ladies to complete the make-up ASAP so that I can get free from there. I started moving my body as per their instructions again cursing Bhaggu in mind for not sparing me even till the last moment.

Finally I was fully ready with that bridal attire but still not sure, if I will actually get married today or not. I could not leave the parlour alone in that attire so had to wait there for someone to come and pick me up. I called Nitin again to check the progress.

BC gayab hai wo tent wala..... khud karwa raha hun sab kaam ek ek worker se yahaan aake, he shouted with all the ill-words he got in his mind for that tent house owner.

159

Were not you and Kamal in touch with him since morning, I asked?

We were, that's the reason we don't have locked banquet here. Till afternoon they were working fine as we were after them to get things done. We got busy with other works at home after that and this is the result now. If I find that bastard owner, I will kill him right here.

Swear yar. How was he reacting when we gave him the contract "she is like my own daughter, I may add on few services from my side for her but you will not find anything missing. I will not let you people down, blah blah blah"

I remember. Worst thing is even stage is not ready yet. Anyways, you chuck it, don't spoil your make-up. We will get the things done.

Fine but they are going to close the parlour. Where do I go and wait? Even the garland vendor will not be available if we don't collect garlands in next 15 minutes.

You try to get it collected from someone as that vendor is very near to your parlour. I will try to pick you as soon as possible.

I spoke to the parlour owner and explained my situation. She sent her office boy to collect garlands and even kept her parlour open even after all the workers left so that I can wait for Nitin there. I so wanted to talk to Arjun about this problem for he might suggest some solution but I did not call thinking he might be busy and someone else can answer his phone.

I called my sisters to check what they were up to and found even they were waiting in another parlour for someone to pick them. I asked them to wait there so that when Nitin comes we together can pick them all, they agreed. I was talking to them when I noticed a call in waiting, it was of Arjun. I instantly swiped the calls.

Send me a selfie no, I want to be the first to see you in your bridal look. He said romantically.

I will send that to you later but before that I have a bad news.
Don't tell me this is related to our marriage, please.

This is indeed related to our marriage; I said and told him everything.

We have almost reached the venue, what to do now?

You just make them keep dancing until you get green signal to enter the venue, I requested him and disconnected the call.

I felt bad for him, so sent him a selfie soon after disconnecting the call. He replied back with a kissing smiley and his picture. He was looking dashing in groom's attire. I kept looking at his picture until Nitin called to inform that he is waiting outside the parlour. I stepped out thanking parlour owner for her courtesy. She wished me good luck and I thanked again as this was the thing I needed most at that moment. I had garlands with me already so we straight away went to pick my sisters and from there to banquet hall. We all passed the journey cursing tent house owner.

As soon as we reached the venue I saw Arjun giving poses to the photographer from trestle and all his relatives were dancing madly around him. Nitin parked his car exactly at the gate of banquet and we ran inside the banquet so that people don't get to see the bride.

Most guests left after dinner, few of them commenting on some or the other dishes. I was getting bored in the room I was asked to sit and wait. People kept visiting me there as if it was a museum and I was a show piece. My cheeks started hurting after giving smiles to hundreds of people out of which utmost were unknown to me. I asked Mansi to check how much time it will take for me to be called by the elders for Jaimala. Mansi came back with good news and my sisters including cousins to take me along with them.

I was walking so fast in the excitement that I forgot to behave like a bride until my sisters asked me to behave like one. Finally I was on stage with Arjun which felt like being on cloud 9 with him. He held my hand and took me to the center of the stage and whispered in my ear "I have a bad news". I could have fallen from the stage hearing this but somehow managed to stand straight and asked in lowest voice possible "what's now?". Before he could answer my sister Deepti came on stage and told me that stage is weak and hence we should be careful. I looked at Arjun and he made a face that said "that was the bad news I was going to share".

I had recently seen a funny video of a marriage where bride and groom fell down from a moving stage while groom was trying to put garland on bride who was being hoisted higher by her relatives, making it difficult for groom. It made me even frightened thinking it can happen with me tonight. I was sure that Arjun too must have got that video in his mind as I only had sent that video to him for a laugh. Deepti tried her best to let minimum people go on the stage together. We spent more than 2 hours in grinning like monkeys for the photographers, after that dinner was arranged for members of both the families. I was feeling too hungry as I could not eat well during lunch as I had too many things to do since morning.

Just when I was deciding what to eat first, I was told that as per Arjun's family bride cannot intake salt before the marriage. I looked at Arjun and he said sorry through his sign language. I felt like telling them all that just 3 hours before I was eating snacks in the room I was sitting but kept quiet as the situation demanded.

After few more hours of chanting mantra, I was to wear yellow saree that Arjun's family had brought. My sisters took me to the room so that I can change from that prickling heavy lehenga to this yellow saree. I came down and sat next to Arjun, he winked looking at my changed looks. Finally after a long night, everything was done smoothly and small cold fights of both the pundits (ours' and Arjun's) which didn't matter much as we were finally married to each other.

As the last step of a marriage it was time for farewell ceremony where relatives cry like they have lost the bride forever but in my case, my family and friends knew that I am not going with Arjun and family permanently and that I will be back by evening to mom's home for Kamal's marriage so nobody got tears even after forcing their eyes to produce some. Photographer came to me and requested to shed some tears so that he can click some pictures to complete his album with sad pictures of farewell. I hugged my family members, friends and close relatives thinking it might make any of us sentimental and cry but unfortunately it didn't work as we all knew we are meeting in evening again and going to have a gala time enjoying my brother's marriage so unfortunately I don't have any sad picture in farewell section of my wedding album.

No accidents after that, thanks to Bhaggu. Two days later,

after enjoying Kamal's wedding we left for Mumbai and lived 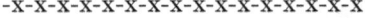 _____ ever after.

To know was it happily or unhappily, wait for the next book.

-X-X-X-X-X-X-X-X-X-X-X-X-X-X-X-X

ABOUT THE AUTHOR

Pratibha Mishra, basically belongs to Ranikhet (a beautiful place in Uttarakhand) but has spent most of her life in Delhi. She is a post graduate in Public Relations & Advertisement. She has served few Multi-national travel companies in Delhi before moving to Mumbai. She recently got married and now lives happily with her husband in Mumbai. She is serving another travel MNC in Mumbai at present. She loves traveling and has traveled to many states of India and few other countries. Apart from traveling, watching movies, writing and reading she just loves dancing and listening music of all sorts. "He loves me... he loves me not" is the first book of Pratibha Mishra.

She can be contacted on pratibhamishrat@gmail.com